3 9077 03078911 2

P9-DDI-034

RAINBOW
MAN

Other Tor books by M. J. Engh

Arslan
Wheel of the Winds

RAINBOW MAN

M. J. ENGH

A TOM DOHERTY ASSOCIATES BOOK
NEW YORK

1-9112

RAINBOW MAN

Copyright © 1993 by M. J. Engh

This book is printed on acid-free paper.

A Tor Book
Published by Tom Doherty Associates, Inc.
175 Fifth Avenue
New York, N.Y. 10010

Tor® is a registered trademark of Tom Doherty Associates, Inc.

Edited by David G. Hartwell.

ISBN 0-312-85468-4

First edition: May 1993

Printed in the United States of America

0 9 8 7 6 5 4 3 2 1

To my brother
(experimentally)

RAINBOW MAN

≈ 1 ≈

We know as a fact that it is right for some people to suffer. The only question is, which ones.
— *From* Revised Manual for Selectors, *Working Draft, Introduction.*

I was the Rainbow Man. On the planet Bimran, people wore shades of gray and brown and white and black, with the occasional daring touch of salmon pink. They weren't used to somebody with clothes like mine wandering around loose. There were offworld tourists, of course, but they came in flocks, shepherded by a tour guide, and didn't stay long.

"Things are free and easy on Bimran," the Migration Control officer told me. "We have no laws."

"You mean no laws for visitors?" I asked, puzzled.

"No laws," said the officer.

Maybe not, but they had regulations. To travel without a tour guide required a visitor's permit, and that meant an interview with a live Migration Controller.

"What is your name?" he asked politely. Every Bimranite I'd seen so far was polite.

"Trojan nine zero eight Liss. No, cancel that. My name is Liss."

"Are you fertile?"

"I beg your pardon?" I said.

He looked at me blankly. "Are you physiologically apt to bear children?"

Physiologically apt—a marvellous phrase. "To bear children? No, I am not."

"Why not?" This seemed a bit personal. But I'd been on planets where the Migration Controllers (or tourist inspectors, or whoever you had to get past before you could start enjoying their world) asked you the color of your great-grandparents' eyes and stuck probes into all sorts of places to measure body odors.

"Because I've been surgically sterilized," I said. "It would take some serious regeneration to make me fertile again."

The officer stroked his console, and with a small sigh it delivered a bright yellow card. He handed it to me. "Verify this now, please."

I looked at it and whistled. "I can tell you one thing wrong with it right away. It says I'm a man."

"Yes?" he said. Still blank.

"I'm not a man. I'm a woman."

"You're an infertile adult human," he said. "That's the definition of 'man.' "

The Linguistic Academy do the best they can, but they can't monitor what every little planet does with their *List of Standard Usages*. I always feel it's a bit of a miracle to get off on still another world and find them speaking (at least around the spaceport) what's recognizably my language at all. Not that it's really so surprising. The *List* they got this month may have left the Academy's regional office no more than a few weeks, or a few centuries, before my ship passed that way. Every *List* is a bubble of language broadcast in all directions from regional offices, swelling outward with the wavefront of last month's *List* just outside it and next month's just inside. Starships glide through the bubbles at all angles, moving not quite as fast, falling steadily behind the unrolling of language. The first thing you get at every port, along with immunization against the local diseases, is a crash course in whatever stage of Galactic Standard they're speaking here. But somehow I'd missed that little vagary with *man*.

"All right," I said, and put the card in my underarm pocket. The Migration Control officer's eyes followed my hand incredulously.

"Keep it with you," he said, recomposing his face into a distant smile. "When you want to renew it, just come back to this office. If you do decide to settle permanently on Bimran, there's no special procedure required. You can simply keep renewing your permit, as many times as you like. Just remember that it's only good for twelve months." That was Galactic Standard Time. It translated into about two years, Bimran local. Such a trifling planet I'd picked, skittering around such a feeble sun. It made you wonder why anybody would bother to colonize it, knowing it could only be good for a few million years. But it was on the starship routes. And I suppose when you're sitting still, a million years looks like a long time.

In whatever world you set me down, I am unaligned, my angles and valences all refusing to mesh with any template I can find there. Contact is a bristly business. Nothing quite fits. And sometimes ("sometimes" equaling "when I'm tired") I long for some all-compassing embrace—the buffering hug that could hold me, prickles and all, the protecting and joining interface between me and a world I could never fit alone. It would be wonderfully comfortable.

Or so I imagine. But something in me bristles at the threat of comfort.

I was born on the Long Haul, and so into a relatively

stable situation. But on the *Trojan*—on any starship, I suppose—our stability was always expectation. We were going somewhere, not waiting for something to come to us. On the Long Haul, meaning any port-to-port lap long enough to be born and die on, we were our own little world, developing our own little indigenous history like any normal planet. Still, we knew we were butterflies, too wing-overgrown to do anything but flit.

But "butterflies" was Doron's word. Better to call us condors, like those live sailplanes of Ishi Two. Those things could have stayed up more or less forever, riding the winds, if they hadn't needed to come down for dinner. But on the ground, blinking their big eyes and dragging those enormous wings half-folded across the beach, they looked like they'd blundered into the wrong world. Even feasting on the stranded floatfish that they lived for, they looked misplaced. You'd see one lift its beak out of a hill of meat, strands of ice-white flesh trailing from its teeth, and look blankly around with that "what am I doing here" expression. And watching one try to get airborne again was good for an hour's entertainment. But when they were up they stayed up. That's what starshippers are like, Ishian condors.

Still, I was born near the end of a Long Haul, so maybe I don't really know how it was. I can't remember a time when people weren't thinking in terms of the next port. I was only ten or so when we moved into the tight cluster of Gemmeus, and from that time on it was one world after another, with sometimes no more than a few months between them. That was when I began to find out about not quite fitting anywhere, though I didn't think of it in those terms. I thought of it as being free from local constraints, having the superior viewpoint, that sort of thing. I'd come to what I suspect is the conclusion of most starshippers: *The locals are the yokels.* They were the ones who spent their short little lives on one little world, or at most two or three neighboring worlds, and then came buzzing around the spaceports to haggle for our cargo and laugh at our equipment and our ignorance of whatever had been happening in local time. From a starshipper's viewpoint, these people had no sense of either time or space, and it would have been smarter for them to keep quiet.

Then we got to the edge of the tight cluster, where it frayed out in loose ends, and there was a three-year lap to think about things. Then there was Bimran.

Even if you're born on the Long Haul, you feel it: there's something inherently temporary about starship life. At the next docking, you can get off. Suppose you do get off, suppose your ship leaves without you, suppose another starship never comes. We talk about starship routes as if they were predictable, and starships do tend to follow in each other's wake, because that's where the known profits are; but every starship is essentially a rover, with no itinerary or schedule except what it makes up as it goes along. It's a shuddery thought, that you might be trapped on a single world for the rest of your life, trapped in a single local time. Getting off a starship is only safe if you know you can get back onto one.

That's what I'd always thought. But I looked around at Bimran, and what I'd been brought up to think of as a trap looked more like a haven now: a single world, a single time.

I knew the risks. It's not unheard-of for people like me to get off one starship, planning to settle down, and get right back on the next one that comes along. We'd had a character like that on the *Trojan*, whom we'd picked up on Gantry Four. Some starships are very exclusive, but most of them cheerfully take passengers and welcome almost anybody who wants to buy in. You don't volunteer to join a starship unless you already have something pretty close to a starshipper's outlook.

And a starshipper's outlook is something the planetbound never quite understand. Every starship is different, with its own customs and jargon and bylaws, but they all have the necessities of space-time in common. If you're a starshipper, you know one thing above all: the world you leave today will have ceased to exist by the time you wake up tomorrow. The people you said good-bye to are dead, as thoroughly annihilated as anything can be in this recycling universe. It's not profitable to form lasting attachments with the planetbound; right away you find yourself attached to a disintegrating corpse. For a starshipper, the only real people in the universe are the ones on your own starship.

All that reverses, of course, when you wave good-bye to your starship and watch it sail off (metaphorically speaking) into a future that could have been your present. As far as your shipmates—former shipmates—are concerned, you're dead now, and that means they might as well be dead from your viewpoint.

I said my good-byes on board the *Trojan*, some of them with fairly vigorous embraces. I didn't want a second round of farewells at the spaceport. Better to ride the last lander down with nobody but the comparative strangers of the docking crew and walk off without looking back. And that was it. One instant I was blinking tears out of my eyes, trying to repress a rush of grief and fear; and the next, my foot hit the spaceport pavement and an absolutely unexpected glee surged up in me. For the first time, after all the worlds I'd visited, I was *here*, really *here*. It didn't much matter that *here* happened to be the planet Bimran.

The finality of it surprised me. On any relevant time scale, there'd be a few more fussbudget hours of checklists and clearances before the *Trojan* pulled out of docking orbit and flashed out of my lifetime. But humanly speaking, it had happened. If anybody on the *Trojan* had me on a viewscreen right now, they were seeing somebody they already thought of as about to die. Light-years were opening between us with every step I took. I was on my own, newborn, with a world to explore.

After all the planets I've browsed around on since I was a child, it still gives me a pleasant shudder along the spine when I look up and there's nothing overhead. It's like being on an extravehicular excursion—except more vulnerable, because you don't have a spacesuit. I rubbed the goose-bumps on my arms appreciatively and lined up with a crowd of other people for a floatcar.

The spaceport lay across the river from the south end of Bimran City, where I'd arranged for quarters. I'd been checking out the city for days now (like taking a glance through the viewport before I jumped into space) and I was already used to curious and friendly stares, already liking Bimranites for their open faces and a style of courtesy so straightforward that on a lot of worlds it would have been rudeness. "Nice day," they greeted each other. "Nice day," they said to me.

Bimran wasn't what you could call a spectacular world, but it struck me as a vivid one. That was mostly air pressure. More oxygen in your blood tends to make everything seem brighter, or sharper, or more staccato. Sound travels faster, and hits your eardrums with a livelier *boing!* The sky was a bright, sharp blue above us. The air was cool, almost shivery.

Behind me, there was a sudden noise that raised prickles

on my neck and arms—shrill, harsh, and torn. Crazy Bimranite machinery, I thought, and looked back over my shoulder.

Other people were looking too, but no one seemed especially interested in what they saw. Two men were supporting
a third, who sagged between them. They shuffled him hastily
past us and into a floatcar, ignoring the people whose turn
it should have been. I saw his face—eyes and mouth gaping
wildly—and that was when I realized what I'd heard had
been a human scream.

The floatcar drifted serenely off. "What's going on?" I
asked, looking around for somebody to answer.

Blank expressions and averted eyes. "He looked sick," my
nearest neighbor offered.

I shuddered. "People get sick like that on Bimran very
often?"

"No, no," somebody else put in. "I've never seen anything
like that before. Look, here's the next floatcar."

≈ 2 ≈

Discretion does not mean concealment. It means consideration for the feelings and the convenience of others. In most cases, it means using reasonable care to avoid making a disturbance.
—*From* Revised Manual for Selectors,
Working Draft, Chapter 1.

imranites were a funny bunch, I thought. They could ignore somebody being dragged screaming from a spaceport, but they got excited about a concert in the park. Of course, the planetbound are a bunch of funny bunches. What can you expect? They don't have a starshipper's opportunities to see the universe. They tend to grow up thinking that their particular tangent is the universal curve.

But Bimran's tangent was a pleasant one. Entertainments of a very public sort were almost literally underfoot—Bimranites walked a lot—and just about everywhere, or at least everywhere I'd been in these first days on Bimran. Musicians and jugglers performed in the middle of walkways, artists wove light sculptures at unlit intersections after dark, and in every open space there seemed to be games going on, with passersby welcomed to join in. Innocent merriment was big in Bimran City.

I liked the feeling of twelve months guaranteed here. Innocent merriment was something I'd been needing. Not that

Bimran months corresponded to my gut feeling of what a month should be. Instead of the neat six hundred hours of Galactic Standard, a Bimran month was twenty-eight Bimran days, which worked out to roughly five hundred and sixty-one hours. (Or five hundred sixty exact, if you used a Bimran hour.) Everything on Bimran was rough. There were more or less six of those months to a local year, but not quite, which meant they were continually tinkering with calendars to make them come out right on average, though wrong in every actual year. People didn't always agree on the date, because of course there was no officially official calendar. But the Migration Control office had one, conveniently reproduced on the back of my visitor's permit, and I figured I'd better stick to that.

"Rainbow Man! Are you going to the concert, Rainbow Man?"

That was a couple of adolescents, hiding behind each other, laughing as much at themselves as at me. They only waited to make sure they'd caught my attention—it took me a minute to realize that the "Rainbow Man" they were yelling at must be me—and scooted away on a footboard. I grinned and waved.

"Yes, do come," a passerby urged me warmly.

Why not? There was a definite current in the foot traffic, and I joined it. An eager crowd was spilling into the big park that split the city more or less in the middle. Golden Bimran daylight, crackling Bimran air. Six or seven sets of musicians were swooping and wheeling over the crowd on not-so-perfectly transparent platforms that puffed out streamers and concentric circles of colored vapor. Slowly moving translucent baffles floated here and there to bat the sounds around. Clumps of people were scattered on the blue-green moss (so they called it) that covered so much of Bimran, while streams and rivers of the footloose surged and eddied between and sometimes over them. I drifted with the rhythm of the crowd, staring back at all the wide eyes that stared at me. The moss was spongy underfoot, like a weave of little springs bouncing you pertly back against the oppression of gravity.

"Rainbow Man, Rainbow Man," voices chanted and crooned around me, more or less in resonance with the music. Groups of three or four, or sometimes twice that, trailed and circled me, sang their greeting, and gave way to others. I couldn't deny the appropriateness; my dark red sheathsuit was overlaid with a fuzz of white crystal threads that fluffed and stirred in every air current and flashed prismatic spectra in every touch of light. I liked light, and the colorful things it does. Optical equipment maintenance had been my job on board the *Trojan*.

A thin person in black—not the matte black that made the bass note in almost any Bimran crowd, but a slick, sleek, wet-glitter black like the ear-piercing semi-sonics just then dribbling down on us from overhead—danced up to me with little sidling steps. "Starship music?" he shouted. His grin looked cannibalistic.

"Not my starship," I shouted back. I've never had some starshippers' problem of not being able to enjoy local music, but definitely this was something I wouldn't have heard on the *Trojan*.

He was bobbing on his feet, playing the air with his fingers. The platform above us whooshed away on a puff of blue wind that tossed my hair, and the sound level dropped like a skydive. "Rainbow Man, Rainbow Man," sang my retinue of the moment.

The person in black danced between me and the closest of them. "Rainbow Man," he chanted, on a very different note. The side of his lip lifted—a smile of challenge or a sneer. "Why don't you want to blend in, Rainbow Man?"

"Why don't you?"

His feet had almost stopped dancing, but his fingers still fiddled with nothing. "That's not an answer," he said.

"It wasn't meant to be." I let myself be carried along by a soft current of the music, helped by the pressure of people behind. He stuck close to me. "Are you a starshipper?" I asked him.

He turned his face up to the sky and uttered a cascade of laughter that ended in a whistle. "Do I look like a starshipper?"

"Not particularly," I said. Around us the music surged louder.

"My name's Sarelli," he said. "I give you that because you've answered one of my questions, and I haven't answered any of yours. Do you want to go somewhere else?"

I went various places with Sarelli, usually laughing, as I did that day. Sarelli enjoyed showing a starshipper around his city. The piquancy of it seemed to please him. About the first thing he volunteered, after his name, was that he had never been off Bimran—"of course." Everything Sarelli said was more or less a sneer, due to a certain quirk of his upper lip. Even on Bimran it would have been easy to get that fixed, so I assumed he liked it. Whatever came out of his mouth had a sardonic tang to it. That was all right with me. Almost by definition I was a nonconformist myself.

"A starship dropout," Sarelli said. "Why?"

"Why not?" We did a lot of that, batting the question mark back and forth like a gravity ball, in memory of our first encounter.

His fingers made thistledown in the air. "You see a thousand worlds you can never be part of. There's only one spot in the universe—one speck—where you can sink your roots into time and space, and that's one particular starship, outside of all normal time and space. And you choose to pull up those roots and throw them into the void. Still say, 'Why not'?"

"How about 'What's the difference?' Ever heard of relativity? What's the difference between your world and mine, except that yours is called the planet Bimran and mine the starship *Trojan*? What's the difference between a planet and a starship, except that one was manufactured?"

"I'll answer that," he said. "A starship encounters planets, which are worlds of its future. A planet encounters starships, which are worlds of its past."

"Yes," I said. "And isn't it better to be going forward than backward?"

"Then why did you get off?"

That was a good question. That was so good a question that I didn't try to answer it; I only laughed. But I knew the answer: I wanted to stop. I didn't want to go on jumping into futures until I hit one that annulled my world, roots and all. Better to rip up those roots here and now, and let my ex-world go skipping merrily on till it annulled itself somewhere down the line.

The first real starships—starships as a starshipper understands them—were refurbished colonizing ships. The thing about a starship is that it's a huge investment, with no return except to the people on board—from the viewpoint of planetbound investors, with no return at all. By the time their ships came in again, not only they but civilization as they knew it, most likely, would be dead and buried. For a starshipper, civilization as other people know it is a very ephemeral thing.

So starships have always been self-contained enterprises, owned and operated by their crews. Those first refitted colonizing ships had proved their usefulness on their first voyages. Plenty of people on thriving worlds saw that it could be done, and decided to try it themselves. Some of the new ships were built or funded by governments, or whatever the locals had instead of governments, and some by the superrich who saw it as a way of buying their own little mobile worlds; but most of them were collectives from the beginning. A few thousand people get together, pool their resources, build themselves a ship, and take off. A lot of people lost everything they had that way, and probably more people died prematurely than we want to know about, but starships in general were a success. If they hadn't been, people wouldn't have kept building them.

"You know what keeps your precious starships going?" Sarelli said. We were climbing the sinuous ramp that led to the top of a high bluff above the river.

"The slud," I said—one of the very few words of outright slang that even the Linguistic Academy accepts. Starshippers can't be bothered to say "sublight drive" every time, and in this case starshippers have the first and last word.

Sarelli laughed. He laughed well, silver chimes of appreciation for all my frivolities. "Continuity," he said. "The curse of evolution. Whatever planet humans settle on, they start looking for the kinds of things that made their remote ancestors comfortable—and they don't find very many of them together on any one planet."

"Lucky for us," I said. "Starshippers, I mean." It was true.

Starships live by the only sound economic principle discovered yet, which is barter. "We load up with oxygen on
Gantry, nitrates on Ishi Two, uranium and water on Palua,
beryllium from the Myrrhus asteroids, hydrogen on
route—"

"And hold tight," Sarelli said, "until you blunder across
a world that's eager to buy at least one of those commodities.
Every world pays a premium for what's dirt on some other.
And by supplying that usually inappropriate demand, and
delivering your long-out-of-date news, you do your bit in
tying the future to the past."

"People love that out-of-date news," I said. "Any bit of
junk we pick up in one tourist market is an irreplaceable
artifact for somebody else's extraplanetary museum." I
scuffed my shoes against the stony slope of the pavement.
"It's a little scary, you know?"

He tossed me a silver laugh. "A timid starshipper? That
would be another stereotype shattered, if I believed you."

I returned his laugh. "Well, we aren't scared, exactly—I
mean starshippers aren't—but there's just always this bit of
apprehension every time you dock. Has somebody cracked
light-speed? If the slud is finally obsolete—"

"You lose your excuse for existing," Sarelli finished. He
snapped the fingers of both hands, sparks of sound in the
crisp air. "Don't worry, Rainbow Man. We're well past the
Optimistic Period of science." It wasn't that everything
amused Sarelli, I thought; it was more that everything would
have amused him if he had deigned to be amused.

"You know about that?" It always surprises me when the
planetbound know a piece of ancient history.

"When the increase of knowledge was exponential," he
said. "I'm a teacher. I know things."

"And for some reason," I said, "it never occurred to anybody that it wouldn't go on increasing exponentially forever and ever. Is that really true, do you think?"

"Is anything in history really true?" He gestured grandly. We had reached the top of the bluff. "Look—you get the best view of the city from here. Right down there, the Park. There's Southtown, where you live. And there's the spaceport, farther out and across the south bridge—see it? Bimran's token connection with your universe."

I turned in a slow circle, shading my eyes against the dazzle of sunlight. Bimran City lay between ridges, a puddle of buildings and streets spread along the river's east bank and slopping over in places to the west. "What's that yellow spot out at the north edge?"

He gave me a puckish look, alien and considering, as if he were sizing me up for a practical joke that might not be funny. "I'll show you sometime," he said. "And over here's the main museum. There's a display there on the Optimists."

"No, thanks," I said.

Sarelli laughed. "Don't scorn them, Rainbow Man. They were no more stupid than other people. They simply thought they'd developed tools of inquiry that were independent of subject matter—which is another way of saying 'valid forever'. And they made the natural human assumption that human minds can understand anything. Or that the universe wouldn't be so rude as to contain anything they can't understand." His lip got away from him, more of a sneer than he generally allowed himself.

I laughed. "Lucky for us they were wrong."

"Is it? Who's 'us'?"

"Starshippers, who else? Do I know Bimranites well enough to say what's lucky for you?"

"No, that you don't," he agreed, and his grin went ferocious. "That you do not, pretty Liss."

I didn't understand Bimran, and I didn't understand Sarelli. We sat on a bridge in the middle of the city, with our legs hanging over the edge of the walkway. Behind us, the sparse Bimran traffic rolled and ambled, half of it footboards even in the vehicle lanes. As far as I could tell, there were few if any private cars on Bimran. There were no barriers, no walls or railings or posts or wires or power fields or air curtains, just a fluorescent stripe on the pavement near each edge of the bridge. The clumsy, the murderous, and the suicidal were free to wander across the guideline. But in fact Bimranites, though they drove and strolled casually, seemed to do it pretty carefully.

Below us, the river sang. "Is that natural?" I asked Sarelli.

"Not to a starshipper," he said sweetly.

I had to laugh. It was true that every river I'd ever seen on any world I'd ever visited had struck me as patently unnatural—great quantities of dirty water gushing along from nowhere to nowhere, rolling randomly over soil and stone, and open to whatever might fall into them. But the ones I'd seen on other planets had run through grooves or ditches, maybe interrupted by the occasional island or sandbank, but otherwise water from shore to shore. The Bimran River—that was really its name—flowed under, over, and through an irregular honeycomb like an enlarged section through a wall panel. Except that this was sleek yellow stone, streaked with black and iridescent purple. The water pouring through those arches and tunnels and slits was a translucent gray-white, and it strummed and moaned and tinkled and whistled and boomed.

"This is the original bimranite," Sarelli said. "That's what the formation is called—just like an inhabitant of Bimran."

"All right, what's bimranite? Is *it* natural?"

He laughed. "Take a river . . . let it fill up with organic mudstone as it slowly goes dry . . . then add the bimranite. It's natural."

"But what is it?"

"Just a volcanic froth that forced its way through the mudstone seams in the old riverbeds. Eventually water found its way back into some of the same channels and stripped out most of the mudstone. This one is glacier-fed. Do they teach you about glaciers on a starship?"

"Very large ice cubes," I said. I had already learned about ice cubes. Bimran was full of curiosities.

He tilted up his face toward the clouds that moved, ponderously as shuttlecraft lifting, against the deep blue sky. His laugh tinkled to the music of the river. "Pretty Liss," he said. He was still facing upward, but he had rolled his eyes sidelong to watch me. "Lovely Liss. Delectable Rainbow Man."

That *man* business had begun to sting me, especially from Sarelli. I'd taken the Migration Control officer's definition at face value—I had no problem with being an infertile adult human—but since then I'd noticed that ordinary Bimranites ordinarily used *man* and *woman* the same way I did. "I'm not a man," I said. "In case you haven't noticed."

He rolled his eyes upward again, squinting toward the bright blue and white, making his lean face more taut than ever. "Aren't you? I wish you weren't."

"Lucky for you, then," I said.

He folded his arms across his chest, digging his fingertips into his shoulders. "My, my," he said mildly. "Aren't you a little devil." His head snapped down and around to view me straight. "Any rainbows on a starship?"

"Lots. I had a prism lamp I was very fond of." I should

have brought it with me, I thought. It was somewhere downstream in time now, somewhere I could never reach.

He didn't acknowledge my answer. "Have you ever seen a rainbow? After a rain?"

"I guess not."

"Lovely," he said. His voice was drier by the second. "Delectable. Unreachable and untouchable. By its very essence, please note." He unfolded himself and swung his legs up to the pavement all in one complicated movement, like a cargo net opening. "Shall we go somewhere?" He reached his hand to help me up. A thin, very live hand. You notice these things more when you don't get much touching. Before he let go, he showed his teeth again. "No offense, pretty Liss, but you don't arouse me sexually. Try it on somebody else."

I managed a laugh. "And to think I could have stayed on the *Trojan*. I wasn't so unpopular there."

"Oh, I'm sure you weren't." His eyebrows repeated the curve of his lip, knowing and nasty. I felt like a child being made fun of according to principles I didn't understand. Sarelli turned neatly on his heel and I followed him.

It wasn't just Sarelli. He was more noticeable, because he got closer to me; but Bimranites as a class treated me very gingerly. Gingerly at best; I'd seen one or two male shopkeepers, who had accidentally touched me in the course of a transaction, wipe their hands and drop the towelet in the nearest recycler. They didn't do that with other people.

Not that Bimranites weren't friendly. "Nice day!" and a sociable smile were what I could expect from any stranger on the street. In crowds, and especially from children and adolescents, I got the cries of "Rainbow Man!"—never threatening, never hostile. If I was looking lost or confused, which I frequently was, somebody would pop up with a cordial

"Can I help you?" and often go out of their way to get me where I wanted to go or help me accomplish whatever I was struggling to do. Bimranites were always ready to chat, always willing to answer questions. But they kept their distance, physically and otherwise. I got the impression they wanted to remain friendly strangers.

I thought it was the not blending in. I even considered buying a demure beige outfit to give blending a try. I thought seriously about that question of Sarelli's, and came up with some answers. I don't blend in because I'm what I am, and you people are what you are. I don't blend in because I'm who I am. Because I'm the way I am.

No, I wasn't going to masquerade as a Bimranite. And I wasn't going to let them scare me (I told myself seriously). My universe had already fragmented. The *Trojan*, with all the years of my life on board, had flashed into a future beyond my reach. The planets I had visited were scattered behind me like shabby little milestones of history; people who had been my age three years ago were dead now; babies I had smiled at were decrepit. I could never catch up with my world again—my places, my things, the people of my genes and my patterns of speech and gesture. They were far downstream in time, and I was marooned on the little stub of a planet I had grabbed in passing. I could leave it if I chose; but I could not get back to where I had been. I couldn't afford to be scared.

Rivers kept turning up in my dreams. The whole crew of the *Trojan* digging a trench with little spoon-shaped tools that sucked up dirt and rock with musical whistles, while I kept trying to dig in the wrong direction and my mother (maybe) warned me that the water was coming. A horizontal cylinder of twisting, opalescent white, moving (or maybe not moving) under the bridge, and Sarelli trying to push me off into it without touching me. A flowing river of stars across the night sky not of Bimran but of Ishi Two, and me and someone I'd loved a lot once rutting happily on the back of a soaring condor (and when I woke, not being able quite to remember who it was). Shooting the rapids of the River Bimran without a bubblesuit, in and out of syrup-yellow caves and coils and hoops, and someone remarking, "There goes another starship."

≈ 3 ≈

Intentions cannot be known. Consequences are unpredictable. Selection must always be based upon actions.
—*From* Revised Manual for Selectors,
Working Draft, Chapter 3.

O n one level, companionship was easy to find here. There was a lot of friendliness going on. It was simple—at least for the Rainbow Man it was simple—to strike up a conversation with a stranger, and within five minutes you could be well into a heated but amicable discussion of the nature of the universe, the best way to cook greenfish, or the hopball game going on in the street around you. At the same time, a lot of subjects just didn't get talked about.

You never really know much about a world before you get there. The slud isn't light-speed, but it's close. You arrive not far behind any messages you may have sent ahead, which doesn't leave time for a lot of preliminary chitchat. Of course, you pick up information about World B while you're on World A, but World A is usually keeping you busy with its own obscurities.

Every world, except for a few isolationists, talks to its nearest neighbors. For practical purposes, the inhabited universe is a chimera of overlapping neighborhoods. Local trade and tourism keep neighbors thinking enough alike to do business with each other, and the news from World Z, way on the other side of the galaxy, gets to World A along with the rest of the electromagnetic radiation. Starships set their courses by rumor, curiosity, and hope, sliding from one stellar neighborhood into another the way you slide from one color of the spectrum to another, without ever crossing a visible boundary. There's only one closed system, and it's called the universe.

You hear grim things about some places, and I'd seen worlds where I wouldn't have left my ship on a bet. But the little I'd heard about Bimran before I got here had made it sound like a pleasant backwater with a population of cheerful stay-at-homes. After some twenty days onplanet, I knew there was more to it than that, but I couldn't tell yet exactly what. Still, grimness was one thing Bimran had no use for. Local society was low on visible hostility and predation, and high on the milder sorts of fun. People turned out in droves, not only for the big concerts, but to sit on the moss and sing songs together, or to watch a meteor shower, or to dance-ski down a hillside covered with yellow snow, weaving in and out through each other's paths like the beams of a light-plaid. They drank, sniffed, chewed, smoked, injected, inserted, and otherwise absorbed a marvellous variety of mild intoxicants and psychedelics. They did a lot of public eating and public speaking, often at the same time.

But there didn't seem to be much sex. Now and then I saw a woman and a man indulging in a moderate cuddle, but never anything steamier. And the cuddlers were always a married couple. On Bimran you could tell.

"They're married, of course," my friend of the day observed, seeing me carefully not staring at a public kiss.

"How do you know?"

"By their wedding rings," he said. "Look."

We were in a restaurant—one of those public eating places that Bimranites fancied, with big arc-shaped tables for twenty people and small round tables for one or two. We were near one end of a big one, looking across the arc at the visibly married pair. "I see they're wearing rings," I said. "What makes them wedding rings?"

"Look." The woman emerged from the kiss, which had been an interestingly long one, and laid her hand over her partner's on the table, back to back. A flash of light jetted between their fingers. They smiled around at the other eaters.

"When people marry," my companion said gravely, "they're given a mated pair of rings." He was watching the happy couple with more than casual interest, I thought. But then, on an unfamiliar world it takes a while to sort out normal reactions.

"It says in the tourist blurbs that Bimran is free and easy," I said. "Are you telling me people don't kiss in restaurants unless they're married to each other?"

The diner on my other side, a young woman who had been eavesdropping in the cheerful Bimran way, expressed her opinion with a snort. "It wouldn't look right, would it?" she said—calling attention to something obvious. My ignorance was always getting that kind of reaction on Bimran.

My friend's mouth puckered in a little smile that looked half mischievous. "And who knows? Perhaps that's a sign that it wouldn't *be* right."

His name was Doron, and he was a beautiful boy. I had met him at another restaurant, earlier that same day, sitting at one of the big tables (star-shaped in this establishment) with empty seats all around him. He was dressed in an especially drab black, and slender almost to haggardness, with a little dark frosting of beard on his cheeks. He looked young and serious and delectable, and I lusted for him at first sight. I had already had enough frivolity and frustration with Sarelli and people more or less like him. I badly wanted a bit of passion in body and mind.

"You're enjoying Bimran?" Doron asked, sounding shy but hopeful.

My heart thumped. That's a physical reaction, but it has its psychic component. "Yes, I am. More all the time."

"May I show you something?" His voice was like his face—sweet, young, and thoughtful.

"I'd like that," I said, and smiled at him.

I had no idea, of course, what I was getting into.

We drank limpet milk and talked about hell. Limpets, on Bimran, were the hard-shelled muscle-balls that clung to the upper rock slopes under the snow. Bimran didn't have mountains worth mentioning, but it did have ups and downs. There was a lot of small-scale vulcanism, and the crags and bluffs above the river valley were cores and seams of weathered basalt—thinly snow-covered at this time of year, which I'd been assured was late spring. Adult limpets were rock-bound, immobile on whatever patch of territory they'd picked out to settle when they were young. The milk they poured into the snow around them seeped downslope, and flocks of little snowfleas swarmed along those tasty lanes to destruction. The lucky ones stopped before they got to the limpet's jaws. It wasn't really a good analogy for planet-bound and starshippers, but the thought did come to mind.

If you blew the snow away from a limpet and tickled it with a stiff hair or fine twig along the downhill side of its bottom edge, it would usually raise itself a little, as if it were straightening its knees, and emit a quantity of clear fluid from under its shell skirt. This was the so-called milk, and the idea was to catch it fresh, which you did in a flat-lipped little vessel made for the purpose, easing the lip just under the edge of the shell. Limpets lived and grew for as long as they could attract enough food to keep them going, and ranged from thumbnail size to wider than the length of my hand. When you'd accumulated enough milk, you sat in the snow and drank it, cool and nectar-sweet and just slightly dizzying. The best fun was supposed to be planting yourself somewhere on a heavily used ski slope, for the pleasure of being whooshed past by skiers. If somebody had told me about it, I would have called it a lot of trouble for a very small thrill. But Doron simply led me to it—"I wanted to show you this"—and I was almost embarrassed at how much I enjoyed it.

We sat halfway down the slope, trusting our backs to the skiers gliding down from the crest of the ridge. The bright blue sky was dotted with white dabs of cloud. We each had a cup of limpet milk.

"Why did you decide to stop on Bimran?" Doron asked me, and added unnecessarily, "I'm interested."

I laughed. "Mostly, it was the first world that came along after I decided to stop. Are you offended?"

He gave me a little glow of a grin. "No, I'm not."

"I like it," I said, "so far. Of course, I almost always like the world I'm in."

Whoosh! A skier shot past us like a concentrated chunk of wind. "I think Bimran's a little crazy," I added, and sipped my limpet milk. "But who isn't?"

Doron's was the sweetest smile I'd ever seen, almost shy but decidedly not timid. "I don't suppose it will impress you much," he said, "if I tell you Bimran is the sanest world I've ever heard of."

"One mind's *crazy* is another mind's *sane,*" I said. "And maybe you're right. What I've seen of Bimran confirms what I've suspected off and on."

"What's that?"

"That people don't just run wild if they don't have laws and regulations—not unless they've been taught that laws and regulations are what keep them from running wild. Bimranites seem to have a lot of fun, but they're very—I guess 'sociable' is the word." Actually I'd been thinking of words like *tame* and *conventional,* but Doron was too beautiful to sneer at.

Wheeroosh! A skier braked and veered just in time to pass us without damage, and sharp snow sprayed my face. Above the ridge, clouds were coalescing, building a great heaped pile that seemed to burn white in the sunlight. "We do have regulations," Doron said. He must be a student, I thought, with a good student's scrupulousness.

"Your regulations are like other people's guidelines," I said. "No teeth in them."

"Teeth?"

"No penalties for noncompliance. And you don't have laws. That's true, isn't it?"

"We don't have laws," he said gravely, "but we have law."

Whoosh! Whoosh! One on either side of us, laughing as they passed. I raised my milk cup in salute. "How do you mean that?" I asked Doron.

"The law of God," he said. "People who respect the law of God have no need for other laws."

"What god is that?"

"The God," he said. "The only God."

I had heard, somewhere out in the Gemmeus cluster, that religion was a big thing on Bimran; but I'd seen so little evidence of it, I'd dismissed that rumor as just one of the things you hear. I'd studied history, I'd experienced a few religious worlds, I thought I knew something about religion; and on Bimran I hadn't even seen anything that could be called a place of worship. "How do you know what the law of God is?" I asked. I put my tongue down deep into the cold sweetness in my cup and looked at him over the rim.

"Oh, it's been documented," he said. "It's not something that could be constructed by either human or machine intelligence. It has to be inferred from actual revelations."

WhoozZZZzzz! That was a skier going straight over us, timing the jump just right. We both ducked, we both laughed, we both drank limpet milk and looked at each other sidelong and laughed again.

"Revelations!" I said. "Does that mean God talking to you?"

"Talking to somebody," he said. When Doron smiled, the corners of his eyes crinkled.

"What happens if you *don't* respect the law of God?"

"But we do."

"I mean, do you believe in heaven and hell and all that?" I was remembering my history lessons.

"Not hell! Hell is a—" He sounded indignant. He seemed to be groping for a word. "Hell is an insulting idea."

"Oh, sorry." It doesn't pay to mess with religious fervor, I knew that much.

He laughed. My fingers itched to touch his little beard, like soft black moss. If he had been any furrier, I wouldn't have been able to resist petting him. "You don't need to apologize to *me*," he said. "It's the people who first imagined hell who owe an apology to God."

"That's good," I said. "I don't think I like the idea of hell myself."

"I didn't think you would." He positively glowed at me—
the sweetest look anybody had given me in years, and I got
it for a point in theology.

"Does that mean," I said, pushing my luck, "you don't
think people should be punished when they break the law of
God?"

Whoosh! Wheeoosh! Whoosh! Three in a row, doing a little
trail-braid down the slope. Doron's face went melancholy—
I'd misunderstood him. "That's not what I mean at all," he
said. "Punishment is designed to make people better, and
therefore happier. It's very appropriate."

"Isn't hell supposed to *be* punishment?"

"So it was claimed," Doron said gloomily. "And still is, I
suppose, by a few sects. Not on Bimran, of course. But you
see, hell can't be punishment."

I laughed in the middle of a sip, spilling limpet milk down
the front of my warmsuit. Doron reached to help me wipe
it off with a handful of snow. "I thought hell was people
burning in terrible pain forever," I said. "Sounds like punishment to me." Doron went barehanded, like a lot of Bimranites. He had nice, small hands, short-fingered, gentle, and
sure.

He picked up the milk cup he had set down, and nursed
it in both his hands. "Pain after death," he said. "When it's
too late for the criminal to repent and reform. Pain that no
living person can witness and be deterred by. No rehabilita-
tion and no deterrence. No benefit either to the criminal or
to the population at large. Hell makes nobody better. Hell
prevents no crimes."

"What's it good for, then? Why did anybody ever believe
in it?"

He swung his head from side to side, which is a Bimranite
gesture of negation. "There's no possible justification except

revenge—and that's no justification at all. But people who felt wronged and outraged and helpless could take some comfort from the thought that those who had wronged them—and wronged God—would suffer. Would suffer horribly, and inevitably, and eternally." He looked at me with wounded eyes. Doron, it seemed, took these things seriously.

"And that makes them feel better?" I shuddered and laughed.

"It's distasteful," he said; "but it's human. What's wicked is to ascribe the same motives to God. Why should an omnipotent, omniscient, loving deity condemn anyone at all to fruitless suffering?"

I ran my hand down my front, where the spilled milk had left sparkles of frost. " 'Fruitless' is the key word, right?"

He nodded his head forward, which is a Bimranite affirmation. "That's it exactly. If any good could come of it, that would be different. But endless punishment after death is useless. Its only function is vengeance. And vengeance is a vicious, childish purpose. It heals nothing; it only returns a hurt for a hurt. God could never be guilty of it!" His beautiful eyes flashed with feeling. Like frost and fire, I thought poetically. Really I could have hugged him, and never mind if it offended Bimranite propriety. But I was more afraid of offending Doron's propriety. Already he had drawn back from his outburst, nursing his limpet milk demurely. "I don't know if you know," he said, with a little smile that make him look wistful; "people don't often choose to sit next to me. I'm a Selector."

"Selector? Is that bad?"

"No," he said seriously. "It's very good. It's necessary."

"What do you select?"

"Individuals. I select individuals for bliss or punishment."

Suddenly he looked different to me. I had no idea what he

was talking about; I didn't realize yet that Bliss and Punishment came with capital letters; but I understood that this delicious boy exercised some sort of authority, that good and bad things happened to people according to his decisions. I wouldn't hold that against him necessarily; but it meant that he was a threat to some people, and I would bear that in mind, just as I would have borne it in mind if he had carried a weapon.

So I laughed. That's one of the things laughs are good for, distancing yourself from a threat. "They told me there are no crimes on Bimran," I said. "I don't see why you need punishment." And only then I remembered that he had used words like *crime* and *criminal* when he was talking about hell. I took a quick drink, hiding my face in my cup. I wished the conversation had never taken this turn.

Maybe he wished the same. He looked down at his own cup. "It's different for you, Liss. We don't select starshippers. We don't select anyone who hasn't been exposed to it from childhood."

"Exposed to what?"

He looked up, faintly smiling. "To the Selection system. Please don't be—don't be alarmed. It's something Bimranites do to Bimranites. You don't ever need to know about it."

I set down my cup. "Yes, I do. Yes, I definitely do."

A crash of sound like the collapse of a wall cracked and rumbled around us. I jerked, knocking over my cup, and the rest of my limpet milk disappeared into the snow. "Slud! What's that?" Aftershocks of noise from no identifiable direction still grumbled around us.

Doron had twisted his slender body to look upslope. "Thunder. We'd better catch a floatcar back to town. Here it comes!"

He sprang up. I was right beside him, with his hand under

my elbow to give me a boost. The great white pile of cloud had turned dark on its underside. A sharp-angled flare of light seared across it, letting loose another crackling bellow. Wind swept down the slope, and flying pellets of water pounded our faces. We turned and ran downhill.

≈ 4 ≈

Belief is not a matter of choice, and therefore cannot be used as a measure of virtue. It would be grotesque to reward or punish people for what they believe to be true. Belief, however, can influence actions, and some beliefs are more conducive than others to virtue. A good Selector will be aware of this.

—*From* Revised Manual for Selectors,
Working Draft, Chapter 5.

Bimran's economy was like a starship's in at least two ways. There was a lot of barter, and nobody worked very hard. I knew of worlds where the dominant motivation of life was to accumulate buying power, and others where just staying alive required unremitting hard labor. On Bimran, it seemed most people had a profession, and on the average they worked at it a few hours a day—in their own homes, or in the shops and schools and cooperatives that Bimran City teemed with. Heavy industry (what little there was of it) was fully automated and underground, mostly in the hills above the river valley.

My personal economy was going to fit right in. I had taken most of my *Trojan* equity in gold, and most of that in skeins of gold thread. Naturally there was no official currency on Bimran—there was no official anything on Bimran. What there was, was a general use of offworld currencies—Ishian especially—and a more-or-less interchangeable multiplicity of "trading media," as they called them—credit systems operated by private companies. I'd used some of my gold to buy credit from a few of these, and banked most of the rest with them for safety's sake (no laws means no police, among other things); but for everyday purposes I bartered as I went. The going rate for gold was one of the things I'd checked before I left the *Trojan,* and I made it a habit to wear or carry enough to cover any expenses I was likely to meet in the course of a day. Bimran wasn't as metal-poor as most worlds in the cluster, but gold was still a rarity here.

"Pretty stuff," Sarelli said. His fingertips just flicked the loose twist of gold I had hung around my neck as decoration and ready cash.

"It's vacuum-spun," I said. "Stronger that way. Do you want some?"

"Are you offering some?"

"What do you have to trade?"

His sharp smile came and went, like something deep in a river pool. "Technique, Rainbow Man. Shall we do business?"

I laughed. "Well, there are techniques for everything. What is yours good for?"

His eyebrows arched. "Physical—comfort," he said, dragging it out.

"Ah, come on, don't tease me, Sarelli."

"Tit for tat," he said cheerfully. "But I do teach basic healing, if you're interested in an honest exchange."

"Why not?" It kept coming over me at unexpected moments, like a program-interrupting announcement: *You are here for the rest of your life.* Unless, of course, I wanted to throw another world down the disposal chute. I was here, and I might as well make the most of the local facilities, Sarelli included.

"My fees are competitive," he added.

Sarelli wasn't a history teacher, as I had imagined. He made his living teaching intermediate reconstructive bio-feedback—meaning how to heal your own internal lesions. Things that other people did by nanotechniques, Bimranites liked to do by manipulating their own physiology. Most people here learned the basic techniques of controlling blood flow and replacing surface tissue while they were still in the skinned-knee stage of childhood, so Sarelli's students were usually adolescents, or older folks refurbishing their skills against the onslaughts of time.

In my case, the first thing was adjusting my circadian rhythms to the Bimran twenty-hour day. We'd used the standard twenty-five-hour on the *Trojan,* and I was still get-ting hungry and sleepy at all the wrong times. It's one of the reasons a lot of starshippers don't bother to get off on any of the planets they dock at, or don't stay off more than a few hours at a time. You're almost guaranteed to be out of synch. Except on worlds like Namsatt Nine, of course, where the planetary day is several years Galactic Standard and people fall back on the twenty-five-hour system. Imitation starships, a friend of mine called them once. But not very good imita-tions. Most of the crew on most starships would rather visit another docked starship than go exploring onplanet any farther than the spaceport. Planets are too unpredictable. Personally, I like that.

Sarelli gave me lessons in the Park where we'd first met, casually scheduled for every second or third day. As often as not, they ended with one of us saying, "See you for dinner?" and the other answering, "Meet you here." We would eat, and drink, and play games, and wander around Southtown and the Park, and everywhere we talked.

"Sarelli, may I ask you a question?"

He turned a howl of silent laughter to the stars. "Do you ever do anything else?"

"No, I mean it. I'm a stranger here, I never know what may offend people."

"I'm not easily offended. Ask it, Rainbow Man."

My gaze drifted around the open-air drinkshop where we sat, side by side on a bench whose broad armrests served a dual function—as a place to put your drink and elbows, and as a separation between every two customers. "What's the Selection system?"

"Oh, Rainbow Man! It's Bimran."

"How about a little more definition?"

He lifted his drink tube, his fingers playing it like a flute. "All right. The principle is very simple. Some people meet our standard of behavior; some people violate it. We reward them appropriately."

"So how do you tell those people apart? What's your standard?"

"That's simple too. Cultures that accept the reality of God can be identified by their moral code. That *is* the standard, Rainbow Man."

"Oh, slud, Sarelli! I've seen as many moral codes as I've seen worlds. Moral codes are the rules people work out for living together, right? And every society has its own. Some places, it's immoral to live with your siblings; others, it's wicked to move away from them. On Ishi Two, it's immoral to fight; on Ishi Three, fighting is the only way you can prove your virtue."

His mouth quirked. "Yes, aren't there some bizarre moralities in the universe? But if you leave out the ones that deny God, and subtract the minor variations, there's a core morality left over. We call it the Commandments. It turns up on dozens of worlds—even unrelated worlds. The only things they have in common are the same basic morality and the same belief in God."

I took a slow sip. "I guess I can believe that. I mean, odd patterns do turn up." Actually I was thinking of the starship pattern, which only looks odd from the surface of a planet. Starshippers are alike the way river pebbles are alike; it's the rolling that does it. But planets are supposed to be different. "So where do those things come from—the morality and the belief in God? How do you get them?"

He laughed, bright and splintery. "How does a child get a basic education? It's given to you, whether you want it or not. We're not sure how many separate revelations there have been, but it seems to be a very small number—beginning with the original one on Earth."

Revelations again, just as Doron had told me. I frowned at my drink. "Aren't there people all over the inhabited universe who hear voices and that sort of thing?"

"You'd know that better than I, wouldn't you?" But he eased up a little. "Yes, of course. The problem was always to distinguish revelation from multiple personality and hallucination and fraud and telepathy and misinterpreted dreams. That's what the morality analysis did; it showed how consistent the Commandments are and how they correlate with monotheism. Really with nothing else."

"Wait a minute, Sarelli. You're telling me your God created your morality? Invented it, decreed it, whatever?"

His mouth opened in a silent laugh. "Revealed it, Rainbow Man."

"You mean the only reason anything is morally good or bad is that God says so?"

He cocked his head. "That's a way you could put it."

"Now, *that's* bizarre! You think if people don't believe in your God they don't have any morality at all? I'm going to resent that, Sarelli."

"Are you?" He drained his drink and bounced to his feet. "Shall we go somewhere? Run? Dance? You can work off your resentment."

On the *Trojan*, I'd had a collection of river pebbles from a dozen different worlds—smoothed a dozen different ways, but with a couple of really odd shapes among them. I stood up slowly. "Sarelli, what does it mean when it takes two people to get somebody into a floatcar at the spaceport?"

He laughed silently. "Is that a riddle? Are you offering prizes?"

"No, I'm serious. It's something I saw the day I left the *Trojan*. I think something was wrong."

"Something certainly was wrong. Too much luggage? Paralysis? Fear of floatcars? If you wanted to know, pretty Liss, why didn't you ask on the spot?"

"I did ask. Nobody wanted to answer. All I got was 'He looked sick.' "

"Then I rather imagine he was sick." Sarelli's eyebrows mocked me. "It does happen, Rainbow Man. Technique can't cure everything."

Bimranites were suckers for pretty things. They might not wear anything flashy—in fact they didn't seem to go in for any form of conspicuous consumption—but they loved toys. The air of Bimran, at least in the city parks, was generally full of boomerangs and whirligigs and music, and the shouts and laughter of games that proved *low-tech* doesn't mean *simple*.

I had a little hand loom that could weave almost any kind of filament into almost any three-dimensional pattern. By way of advertisement I spent a sunny morning in the Park, weaving stars and balls and strange attractors, ethereal puffs and butterflies of gold the size of my open hand, and incidentally keeping an eye out for a slim figure in dull black. I hadn't seen Doron the Selector since that first and apparently last day when he'd introduced me to limpet milk and the immorality of hell. But I was still looking.

I took it on trust that Bimranites would find some use for my weaves, and they didn't disappoint me. I hadn't finished my fourth when a crowd of people who announced themselves as the Puffer Club bounded up to me, squeezing syringes that made pathetic little farts of noise. The sport of puffing, it seemed, consisted of keeping a ball in the air by blowing it back and forth with these things. The Puffers were enchanted by my golden fluffballs. "How much? How much, Rainbow Man?" They were all around me, bouncing on their feet, squeezing and squawking their syringes, puffing their swirl-striped ball back and forth over my head.

"Ten days' rent in Southtown," I said, loudly enough for the whole flock to hear me. I'd very quickly learned this style of expressing exchange value. On Bimran you didn't have to buy or construct your own living quarters, as on some worlds, but neither were they supplied by any central housing authority. It was up to you to find vacant lodgings or someone willing to share space with you. Either way, you paid the building's owner a fixed rate which they called "rent." The city of Bimran fell into unofficial but very clear sections, and within any one of them rents tended to be so standardized they could serve as a medium of exchange. Everybody knew what ten days' rent in Southtown amounted to: about twice what it would take to live in Northtown but less than what you'd have to pay in Parkside or Riverside.

"Ooh, that's a lot. . . . That's too much for a toy." The Puffers drew back from me a little, smiling and considering.

"Here, try it out." I tossed them a golden nova, and half a dozen squirts of air caught it and sent it spinning. The Puffers capered away, with cries of delight. I watched them gambol across the open, chasing the flash of gold around trees and over flowerbeds and under rain shelters. In a few minutes they were back, one of them balancing the weave on her palm and the rest of the club massed quietly behind her. "Seven days Southtown?" she suggested.

We struck a bargain at four weaves for thirty-five days, and we all trooped off together to pay my rent at once. That was my stipulation, as partial safeguard against the hazards of a totally unregulated economy. I didn't want to accept a string of assorted currencies from the Puffers and then be told it would only pay for fifteen days.

If I had needed any more publicity, the walk provided it. The Puffers kept their new playthings on the fly, darting sunbursts that bobbed and sparkled merrily through Bimran traffic. The whole club was in euphoria, whooping, singing, and telling everybody within earshot that they got their pretties from the Rainbow Man.

My quarters were in a typical Southtown structure—a little, low loop of a building, made of something hard, brown, and opaque, with the doors of the apartments opening off the narrow central court. The landlord was a soft-spoken old person with a bit of an impish twinkle peeking through his shy look. He accepted the payment and changed the date on my doorkey while I watched. The Puffers thanked me profusely and bounded off.

One of my neighbors, in the process of entering her own quarters, had paused to observe the whole transaction with frank curiosity. As soon as the landlord had handed me my revised key and closed his door, she let out a loud snort of amusement. "You didn't need to do that, girl. They're honest." She waddled forward, holding out her right hand in the immemorial starship greeting. "Leona Porlock, formerly of the *Bedouin*. And you're from the *Trojan*. Come in and sit awhile." Her broad face split with a grin. "I'm fat and I'm old and I'm rude, but I'm a starshipper. Come on."

If Sarelli gave me a Bimranite view of starshippers, Leona Porlock gave me what I needed more right now, a starshipper's view of Bimran. On the whole, it was encouraging.

"I suppose there are more reasonable planets," Leona said. "But I'm comfortable here. I like the climate, for one thing. Hated it, at first."

"Did you?" I said. "I liked it from the first sniff."

Leona laughed. "I'm heavy enough at one gee—I don't need the extra ten percent. A skinny little thing like you, it doesn't matter. And the air pressure bothered me. But then I started noticing I was more comfortable than I'd been in years. More energy. It's the extra oxygen does it, and the ion concentration."

"I used to know a song about negative ions," I said. *"You got to ac-cen-tuate the negative, Dis-crim-inate the positive . . ."*

"And it's cool," Leona said. "Never gets up to sweating temperature on Bimran. I appreciate that. It's worth a few thunderstorms."

"I love the thunderstorms," I said.

It was true about the oxygen and the energy and so on. But Bimran, in spite of the coolness, seemed somehow tropical to me. The heavy air felt sultry—sultry but dry, like a model jungle built for tourists who wouldn't pay to sweat. The air was supercharged, always preparing itself for the next lightning stroke. Whatever you saw or heard or tasted on Bimran seemed portentous, whatever you said or did throbbed with significance. Maybe they didn't need bright clothes here.

Everyone said "Nice day" but no one except Leona Porlock had ever said "Come in." No Bimranite except Sarelli had even shown an interest in seeing me more than once. And though Sarelli seemed pleased to show me the sights of Bimran City, such as they were, and to take me on as a student, I noticed that we never went anywhere that might be called private. Our lessons were always in the Park.

Learning to sleep on schedule hadn't taken long. Sarelli was a good teacher; he made it almost as simple as resetting my watch and tucking it back in my ear. But we'd kept on with the lessons. Now I was learning to do things for myself that on the *Trojan* we'd done with a little drop of something on the tongue or maybe a few strokes of a purrcat. Some of it was easy. Heartbeat, blood pressure, breath were things even a starshipper could control with a little practice. Tissue repair would take longer. "Remember that you're a unified system," Sarelli told me patiently. "Your conscious mind connects directly or indirectly with everything that happens in your body. You can *tell* those corpuscles where to go."

"And how do I know if they listen?"

He laughed. "When you learn to feel it, you'll be qualified to join my regular class. Ready to try the blood flow exercise again? Good for headaches and blushes."

Learning to feel at home in my own circulatory system was a lot like learning to feel at home on Bimran—not as simple as I'd expected. I still wasn't easy enough with Sarelli (much less with any other Bimranite) to ask him about the way Bimranites reacted to me. But Leona Porlock was a starshipper.

"Send me away if you've got other things to do, Liss. I'm on my way to get a bite to eat, and I thought you might like to join me."

"Now, *that's* refreshing! Come in and sit down, Leona. Just let me change my clothes."

She settled herself into a seat—one of the standard pedestal poufs that Bimranites called mushrooms, which molded themselves cozily around your buttocks and back. "Bimran on your nerves already?"

"I suppose so." I was rummaging through my wardrobe for something Bimranly warm but fun to wear. "The thing is, Leona, I meet people, we have fun for an hour or two, and then that's the end of it. Even Doron didn't say anything about seeing me again."

She gave me a shrewd look. I had told her about the limpet milk. "What's this 'even Doron' business? Did he give you any reason to expect he would?"

"He spent most of a day with me. Doesn't that mean anything?"

"Means he had most of a day free."

I found my green-slashed puffsuit and began to put it on. "He's a Selector," I said. "Is that good or bad?"

She snorted. " 'Good or bad'? You sound like a Bimranite. It's like most things a person can be—complicated."

"He's very emphatic about God," I said.

"They have a lot of God here," Leona said unsympathetically. "If you ask me, they'd be better off with a lot of gods."

"You don't like monotheism?"

"No, of course I don't. It goes against common sense. If you really want to hypothesize any kind of supernatural stuff going on—I mean any kind of spiritual entities, whatever those are, affecting material events somehow—well, the obvious conclusion sure as slud isn't that there's one stupendous mind running everything. What the universe looks like—at least what it looks like if you don't sign on to somebody's grand unified ready-made theory before you open your eyes—"

"Not me," I said. "I've seen too many theories go down the disposal chute."

"You and me both," Leona said. "Any starshipper has. And what the universe looks like to common sense is a lot of independent, unequal, unaligned forces just knocking around together. Which is how people always saw it back on old Earth, until they got civilized and too smart for their own good. And another thing—"

I laughed, delighted with her vehemence. "So, back to nature and polytheism? What's the other thing?"

She gave a grudging grunt. "It wouldn't be so bad if people would stop with just postulating a single deity. But no, they generally go on and start calling it good. That's where the real harm comes in."

I laughed a different way. This was almost intruding on Doron's space. "How do you mean that?"

"I mean," Leona said, "if you appoint one big God and give it credit for everything, you have to give it credit for *everything*. If God made flowers, God made shit."

"So what gods do you recommend?"

Leona made an explosive gesture, taking in a good part of the known universe. "Doesn't matter much. Doesn't matter at all, in principle. You can personify any old aspect of the world that takes your fancy—or that worries you—and you can worship it however strikes you as appropriate. Me, I'm an antiquarian by preference. I've dug up some of the old gods from Earth. I say my prayers generally to Athena and Hermes and Rab."

"I think I've heard of Athena," I said doubtfully.

"So you should have, if you know any Earth history. She was the patron of the city of Athens and pretty much the inventor of civilization. Goddess of wisdom is what she is— wisdom meaning how to *do* things, not any metaphysical stuff. Which is why I like her. She's a tough goddess. In the old Greek system, Ares was the dumb war god, the one who always said, 'Oh, boy—a fight!' But Athena handled the strategy and tactics. And a very protective deity. She takes care of me." A serious note in her voice there, and she tucked her chin down into the rolls of her neck with a decided little jerk.

"Sounds like somebody I could use," I said. "Who did you say the others were?"

"Hermes is the god of travelers—a natural for a starshipper. Also the god of luck and double-dealing and all the stuff that Athena wouldn't stoop to. And a trickster—the only Greek god with a real sense of humor. The god of quantum mechanics, in my opinion. Remember quantum?" She laughed her wide-open laugh. "Now, Rab's not Greek. I picked Rab up on—what was the name of that planet? I didn't think I could ever forget it." She looked older for a minute, withdrawn into the privacy of her vexation. "Well, never mind." (Emerging on a spurt of energy.) "Rab is a useful little deity. I've gotten very fond of it. Sometimes she's female, sometimes he's male, but mostly I think of it as an it."

I laughed. "What's it in charge of?"

"Mistakes. It's the deity of getting some sort of profit out of your own mistakes. Other people's too, of course, but that's just taking advantage. Rab is in charge of taking advantage of yourself. Handiest little dickens!" She sank into a jouncing chuckle.

"I haven't heard any god stuff on Bimran at all," I said, "except from Doron. Well, and a little from Sarelli. But I certainly haven't noticed people doing anything religious."

Leona sniffed. "That's because of what Bimranites have done with religion."

"What's that?"

"The same thing a lot of reformers and protesters and theologians have tried to do a few thousand times elsewhere. They've taken the ritual out of religion—made it strictly an intellectual and moral thing. And you know, if they'd asked my advice, I'd have said that's a dumb mistake."

"At least like this it doesn't get in people's way." I snuggled my chin into the puffsuit's swelling front and patted my sides through its rotundity. "Where shall we eat?"

Bimran was a do-it-yourself world. If you wanted to eat, you went to a restaurant or snackshop, or else you went to a food shop, bought some raw materials, carried them back to your quarters, and constructed your own meal.

We headed north along one of Bimran City's not quite straight thoroughfares. The main streets meandered north and south in more or less regular harmony with the river—sometimes curving, sometimes angled—and shorter connecting streets splayed across them in all directions.

"I tried a footboard once," Leona said. "Toxic thing slid right out from under me." She chuckled heavily. "And let me tell you, when I come down on a Bimran pavement, I come down hard!"

"Yes, what is it about this place?" I stamped my foot. "Listen to that! Whoever heard of hard pavements, except on Bimran?"

"You just put your finger on it, Liss—your foot, anyway.

Hard and impervious. They might as well use rock. In fact, they do use rock, a lot of times. Bimranites like things hard."

"But why?" I kicked at the unyielding surface, perversely savoring the pain in my toes. "Are you sure it's not just technological backwardness?" Starshippers get to say that too, sometimes. A lot of worlds have regressed, by choice or by accident, or gotten stuck at a certain level of development.

Leona pursed her lips. "Some of that. The Bimranite position is, Why should they be interested in technology if their God isn't? But they've got a normal pavement at the spaceport—normal permeable on top of normal filtering. No, I think Bimranites just like things hard."

"How long have you been here, Leona?"

"About twelve years local." She eyed me humorously. "If I can do it, Liss, you can do it. Come on." She linked her arm with mine, and we strolled on. "I wouldn't be a Bimranite for all the plutonium on Ishi Three," Leona said. "But it's a pretty good place to be a resident alien. I've made some good friends here." She shook with seismic laughter. "They think I'm a terrible sinner, of course. But the thing is, it's all right for *me* to be a terrible sinner. They don't hold it against me."

"Speaking of spaceports—" I almost stopped in my stride, the scene came back to me so starkly. Leona's solid bulk hauled me forward. "I saw a funny thing the day the *Trojan* left. Somebody getting dragged into a floatcar with a very strange look on his face. I think I heard him scream, Leona."

She grunted. I got back into step, and we walked on. "Oh, slud, Leona!" I said. "Aren't *you* going to answer either?"

"You didn't ask me a question."

"What happened? What was it? That's a question I'm asking."

"I wasn't there," she said judiciously. "But it sounds to me like a Bimranite got caught trying to leave the planet."

"What do you mean, caught? Who caught him?"

"The authorities, who else?"

"I thought there weren't supposed to *be* any authorities."

She snorted a laugh. "You've got it wrong, Liss. There's no government, no armed forces, and no police. But there's a Migration Control Service, which is nearly as bad." She cackled. "There are quotas for how many offworlders they allow on Bimran. Did you know that? So many starshippers per year, so many total living immigrants and visitors at any one time. They don't tell people that; but if you'd tried to enter when the quotas were filled, they'd have found reasons to keep you out. They don't want the moral dilution."

"The what?"

"Moral dilution. That's what they call it. Too many unbelievers mixing with the faithful."

I laughed. "Oh, right! Like a very fragile ecosystem. But are you telling me they don't let people out? Are they afraid of depopulation?" I could believe that. There were only a few million people on Bimran all told.

Suddenly she looked old and humorless, a strange expression for Leona, or at least Leona as I'd known her. Her eyes met mine—faded old eyes that had seen worlds that were dead before I was born. Starshipper's eyes; we might have recognized each other in a crowd on any world in the galaxy. She blew out her breath in a grim chuckle. "Well, you and I can go any time we want to. But they don't let Bimranites leave."

I wasn't laughing now. "Why not?"

"They can't," she said. "If they did, there'd be a way out."

I'd heard of people's necks prickling, a good old mammalian alarm response, but I'd never felt the sensation before. Yes, I had; once, at the spaceport. "Bimranites don't act like people who feel trapped," I said.

"When people really feel trapped," Leona said, "they don't fight it."

≈ 5 ≈

For every individual, the past determines the future. This is another way of saying that we choose what will happen to us. A Selector must never feel remorse.

> —*From* Revised Manual for Selectors,
> *Working Draft, Chapter 1.*

I really do enjoy planetary atmospheres. You get wind and all those interesting meteorological phenomena, and the smells are an entertainment in themselves. I loved the Bimran sunsets and the gorgeous Bimran thunderstorms. But you can get tired of being buffeted by air masses and drenched by falling liquids. And of course the main problem with those balmy breezes is that they're full of things, most of them allergenic and almost all of them prone to settle out. If you live in a planetary atmosphere, you live with dust. A day or two in the clear, bracing air of Bimran, and any immobile object was filmed with powdery stuff you could draw lines through with your finger. Even indoors, where you'd expect more control. It's one of the things that the planetbound accept as part of life.

"Why the shudder, pretty Liss?" Sarelli asked me.

I looked at my fingertips. "Unfortunately I remember now and then that this is what we're breathing."

He tossed his head back and laughed at the bannerswagged ceiling. "It's what human nasal passages evolved to cope with. Give the cilia something to do or they feel unwanted. Although—" he looked down at the mark my fingertip had drawn— "some of these displays could use a little more dust-repellent." He aimed one long finger like a surgeon's laser and crossed my line with his own. "X marks the spot."

"Where our paths crossed in the dust," I said, and shivered again. "Well, it doesn't seem to be immediately fatal."

He grinned. "Dust poisoning? No, Bimranites live a dreadfully long time."

"It must seem dreadfully long if they spend much of it in places like this. Let's look at something that moves."

We were in the Bimran idea of a museum—nothing I would have called displays at all, just a building full of *things*. It was one great hall partitioned into a labyrinth by hanging screens, beneath which you could see the feet and ankles of other wanderers following other paths through the maze. Walls, floors, and screens were laced with bright bands of more colors and patterns than I cared to count, and the long festoons above us were part of the same tangled weave— literal guidelines to lead you through the maze, every one offering a differently tailored tour. We weren't following any of them, though we had each checked out a guidebox at the entrance—"for the sake of appearances," as Sarelli said. His was deep bronze with white center streaks; "Weather and Time," it was called, and I suspected he'd chosen it to match his sleek walkingsuit. My box—"Elements of Bimran History"—was checkered metallic green and gold. Bimranites (Sarelli excepted) might be dreary in their dress, but they knew how to use color for functional purposes.

I had listened to my box at first, and still had the speaker in my ear, but I had deactivated it. Sarelli made better listening than the droning commentary triggered by knots in the green and gold line. "Would you believe," Sarelli asked, "there are three hundred ninety-two distinct tours? Would you believe I've taken every one of them?"

"No, and no. Not without further evidence, and please don't give me any."

His grin looked hungry. "Would you believe one hundred twenty-nine? Would you believe I've taken every one of that number?"

I surveyed the intertwining lines that looped in paint and fabric from roof to screen to floor and back again, that disappeared around corners and re-emerged from cross-corridors. "I can believe a hundred and twenty-nine. How long does it take to do them all? And why should you?"

"How much time do you have?" He scooped a circle of air with one quick hand. "That answers both your questions, doesn't it?"

"Hey, what's *this?*"

"Ah, you've found it, have you? What does it look like?"

"If I knew, would I ask?" I peered closer at the display bubble. "I suppose it might be a document of some sort. Those darker squiggles could be a script."

Sarelli snapped his fingers, a Bimran sign of approval. "Bravo, Liss! It's a replica of a very ancient copy of part of the earliest known revelation."

"Oh, not again, Sarelli! Are you going to talk revelations to me?"

He laughed. "Take my advice, Rainbow Man—never reject a revelation."

I consulted my guidebox. "This is on my tour line. I'm going to listen."

"This is on every tour line," Sarelli said. "I've heard it a hundred and twenty-nine times."

I activated my box. "And Abraham drew near," the voice in my ear informed me, "and he said, 'Will you destroy the righteous with the wicked? Suppose there are fifty good people in the city. Will you destroy them too, and not spare the place for the sake of the fifty righteous? Far be it from you to kill good and bad together! Should the good suffer with the bad? Far be it from you! Shall not the judge of all the world do what is just?' And God said, 'If I find in Sodom fifty righteous, I will spare all the city for their sake.'

"Strictly speaking," a different voice continued, "these words do not constitute a revelation. But they are part of the written tradition that incorporated what we may confidently call the original revelation, since it was received on our species' homeworld before the development of space travel. The Abraham of this passage, an archetypal hero of the ancient Hebrews of Earth—"

I deactivated. "That's amazing," I said. "I've studied that stuff. I didn't think anybody but starshippers would be interested in history *that* ancient."

Sarelli trilled a laugh. "What makes you think it's history that interests us? The revelation is just as immediate for Bimranites as for Hebrews."

"Oh, slud, Sarelli! Do you really think your God told the Hebrews how Bimranites should behave? *That's* where you get your standard of behavior?—from a bunch of primitive animal-herders who thought their sun revolved around their planet?"

"Slightly ridiculous," Sarelli agreed. "Rather like accepting the principles of motion discovered by a louse-infested alchemist in knee breeches and a wig. The really funny thing is that Newton was right. The truth he found was only part of the truth, but it was the part most applicable to daily life on a planet's surface. And it applies as well to Bimran as to Earth."

"So does metabolism," I said. "Come on, let's get something to eat."

Eating was one of the things Sarelli and I did well together. Bimranites weren't serious eaters in the same way as Kossolonians or the bulimics of Patro, who could cram down enough food in an hour to feed a *Trojan* crew member for two days. But nibbling seemed to be a major sport on Bimran. Most people ate four light meals a day, and filled in the gaps between them with snacks and sips. Besides the big restaurants, dozens of little shops catered to the habit, and you could spend most of a day and evening strolling from one to another. There were places to sit and places to stand and places to simply buy a drink or a handful of something edible and stroll on, all while you munched and chatted and eyed the passing scene.

"Have you ever known a Selector, Sarelli? Or is that a stupid question?"

His teeth flashed. "Probably not stupid. Possibly profound—who can say?"

"Then do I get an answer?" We had whiled away hours eating our way back from the Museum neighborhood to the edge of the Park. It was night now, the sky thick with stars and no local light but what came from the shops behind us. Sarelli's metallic sleeves glinted as he turned.

"That could be a Selector," he said conversationally. "Coming out of the sweetshop."

"The woman in black?" She looked reassuring somehow—a kind face, a sensible, sedate style of moving. "How can you tell?"

"I can't. I speculate. To answer your possibly profound question, everyone knows Selectors. No one knows Selectors."

I didn't know any longer what I'd wanted to ask him. I watched the putative Selector make her quiet way into the darkness. "Like museums," Sarelli said drily, "they serve their purpose."

"Not the same purpose as museums, I hope. Or do museums have a purpose besides boredom?"

His laugh and glitter led the way across the street into the shadows of the Park. "You don't like museums, Liss?"

"I don't like boredom. Museums are all right if they're fun. But I don't like being tied to the past."

We threaded between patches of shagginess that in daylight would be flowerbeds, and stood under a sky full of glory. Amusement touched Sarelli's voice like the starlight touching his sleek shoulders. "Isn't the perceptual universe a museum? We know what's happened, not what's happening."

I spun in a circle, floating my arms, hugging the night, the stars, the air full of planet scents. "No! It's happening, it's real, I can taste it."

He had stepped back a little, to give me room. "You surprise me, Rainbow Man. I would have thought starshippers, above all, understood that principle. Look!" He waved a glittering arm at the glittering sky. "We know that twenty-odd thousand years ago people in the region of old Earth were still trying to hold together an interstellar union several hundred light-years across. We know this interesting bit of ancient history because it's the latest news we've received. We know that a mere thousand years ago scientists on Ishkenny announced they were on the verge of achieving faster-than-light communication; but if they had succeeded, we would presumably have heard so before that announcement. We know that approximately . . . ah—" in the faint light I could see that his head had turned and tilted, aimed toward the buildings across the Park from us— "point five microsecond ago, Parkside still stood. And I know that less than a quarter of a nanosecond ago a most remarkable being was standing next to me. We know the past—or parts of it. The present we have to take on faith."

We moved on between the dark flowers—I wasn't sure which one of us had started the movement—and he added, "That's 'remarkable' in the literal sense. Conspicuous." I laughed.

≈ 6 ≈

Certainty of Bliss, like certainty of Punishment, becomes a form of coercion. Individuals should never be absolutely sure that they will be Selected.

—*From* Revised Manual for Selectors,
Working Draft, Chapter 2.

There were two rock-hard, rigid-backed seats in the courtyard just outside my landlord's door, and in sunny weather I often found Leona Porlock on one of them. She made herself comfortable with two or three large cushions—supplied, it seemed, by the landlord himself. His name was Korlo, and he and Leona were cronies. They spent hours chatting and watching the street and the sky, Leona solid among her cushions on one seat and Korlo perching on the other like a wispy projection you might have put your hand through. "What do you talk about?" I asked Leona once.

She made a gesture of easy indifference. "People we see. People we don't see. Weather. Birds. All the worlds I've visited and all the tenants he's rented to. We tell each other stories, that's what it is."

Leona had plenty of time for it. The *Bedouin* had been lucky enough to dock on Old Kossolo when it was simply Kossolo and the borax mines were in full operation, several centuries before the *Trojan* got there. Boron is a very profitable commodity on a lot of worlds, and Leona had stepped onto Bimran with more wealth than she could find a use for here. She would never have to work for a living.

Sometimes other people—neighbors or strangers—stopped to join the chat. Bimranites were prone to this kind of open-air affability. They walked, they talked, and when they had nothing else to do they tended to gravitate to the Park.

There were tiny parks scattered all over the city, but when people said "the Park" they generally meant the big one that split the city into Southtown and Northtown, with Parkside clinging to one flank and the narrow strip of Riverside to the other. A nice place, the place where I'd met Sarelli, the place where I could sell my golden pretties as fast as I could weave them. That's what I was doing on the balmy summer morning that marked the end of my first Bimran month. I had my mind on my loom, not paying much attention to the usual circle of bidders and admirers, when I noticed a slim dark figure among them. I hadn't seen him arrive; he was just *there*, standing quietly behind as many people as possible. My heart bounced merrily, and I skipped a turn of my filament and had to rewind to get the tangle straightened out. I was afraid to speak to him—I didn't know what might scare him off—but I aimed a little smile in his direction, and he smiled back. Doron had a lovely smile.

As soon as I'd finished my golden butterfly and sold it to a restaurant-owner for seventeen full meals and five snacks, to be collected on demand, I folded the loom, slipped it into a pocket of my crimson walkingsuit (chosen on purpose to show off the gold), and headed straight to Doron. He waited for me.

"Nice day," he said, with that luminous smile that made his eyes seem to shine.

"Yes, it is." I would have liked to pat his cheek. His beard would be like Bimran moss, I thought, springy and resilient. Soft but hard. "I could use a drink of something. Could you help me find a comfortable place?"

"Of course." Yes, he really did look glad to see me. "Right over here—I'll show you."

He steered me to a little drinkshop that didn't have tables at all, just thickly scattered mushrooms, comfy but separate. The drinks were served in globes hung from the ceiling by slender chains. We found two unoccupied mushrooms close together and got something warm and tasty.

"I haven't seen you for a while," I couldn't resist saying. "Have you been busy?"

"I thought *you'd* be busy."

"Me? Not likely! I have practically nothing but free time."

"I thought you'd be sightseeing," he said. Bimran innocence. But every world thinks it has irresistible sights to see.

"I've seen a lot of Bimran City," I said. "Nothing else."

His eyes widened. "If you like," he said, "I could show you around Bimran."

I laughed. "Don't you have to work?"

"Not for a few weeks." *Week* was an arbitrary Bimran time unit of seven days. It wasn't even commensurate with their year, which came out to be something like twenty-four and three-sevenths weeks. Typically Bimran. "I just finished a case," Doron added.

There was something so scrupulously neutral in his tone, it made me suspect all sorts of violent feelings just beneath the surface. But I have this bad habit of reading the planet-bound as if they were starshippers. How could I tell what a

Bimran tone of voice was meant to hide or reveal? "A case?" I said. "That means work?" Just conversation, I wasn't prying.

"Yes." His dark eyes stared straight into mine, and it came to me that he probably wasn't trying to hide or reveal anything, he was too busy wondering if I would be nice to him. What was he, some kind of untouchable? Or just a shy boy who needed a little loving?

"Then let's go," I said. "I'd like very much for you to show me around Bimran."

He melted beautifully into a smile. "Tomorrow morning, then? I'll meet you here?"

"Watch out, Liss," Leona warned. "You're glowing." She had left her seat in the courtyard and followed me into my quarters when I came back from the Park, and I probably couldn't have resisted telling her about Doron if I'd tried.

"Nonsense," I said. "It's just nice to have a pretty boy to do things with. It's fun."

"I thought you were getting your fun with your friend Sarelli." Her tone said she didn't much approve of either of them.

"Sarelli is fun," I said. "Usually. But he keeps making these insinuations that don't insinuate anything I can see."

Leona scratched her forehead through untidy gray bangs. "Like what?"

"Well, he doesn't *keep* making them. Just every so often he says something like—oh, like when I said that besides gold I offer services, meaning my weaving, and he said, 'I'll bet you do' with this terribly meaningful look—like making fun of me and accusing me of something at the same time, and I've no idea what."

Leona chuckled. "Sex. They think about sex a lot here."

"Huh? I don't see the connection."

"They think sex is only legitimate in very restricted circumstances."

"Marriage, right? I've already figured that out."

"Right. And marriage is restricted to two people of opposite sex. *And* it's permanent. You can see the problems."

I whistled. "Why do they do that, Leona? Bimranites seem so reasonable otherwise."

"It is reasonable, the way they see it," Leona said. "After all, monogamy is what the human species evolved for."

"I hope that's a joke." I selected a stringy sweetstick from the bunch I'd bought on my way home, and passed the rest to her.

"No joke. That's monogamy with plenty of action on the side, of course. Maximizes gene survival for both parents. Stable family to raise the kids. Female has the male of her choice permanently on hand—and if she sees better genes walking around she can always slip out back for a quick fix. Male can monopolize one female to make sure her kids are his—reasonably sure—and try to spread his genes around the neighborhood for backup. Which gives you selection for monogamy with a bit of promiscuous adultery by males and selective adultery by females." She crunched a sweetstick and contemplated the chewed end. "Of course, we also evolved for digging roots and hunting small animals, and most people figure we've gotten past that stage. But here we are chewing on roots—"

I jerked the sweetstick out of my mouth and looked at it. "Is that what these things are?"

Leona rumbled a laugh. "Washed, sliced, and dried—otherwise just as they come from the ground. Hill farmers grow a lot of them."

"It's good anyway," I said, and chewed again.

Leona nodded, Bimran style. "Same with monogamy. And all Bimran's done is eliminate the side action."

"You can't tell me that part's reasonable."

She chuckled. "Eliminating the side action? Nobody claims it's reasonable. That's the part they say nobody could have figured out by themselves. They got the idea from God."

"But, Leona—" I tugged at a random curl of my hair. A few more discussions like this and I'd be picking up all her mannerisms. "If monogamy and adultery are both natural, what makes them accept one and reject the other?"

"Don't you see it, girl? If this system were one hundred percent natural, it wouldn't be a system. You don't need commandments to tell you to do what you're going to do anyway."

I sucked my sweetstick. "So what do they *do*, otherwise? I mean, besides the monogamy?"

"Ogle and dream a lot. Or else feel very guilty. Or both. And when somebody like the Rainbow Man comes along—"

"Don't Rainbow-Man me, Leona. I get enough of that from Bimranites."

"Just trying to explain, girl. But if it makes you feel better, let's say when an attractive offworlder comes along—an unorthodoxly attractive offworlder—" She shrugged. "They get a bit of a tickle from assuming that you're very wicked by their standards."

I thought it over. "I still don't quite understand. Why is that funny? Funny and—contemptible, I guess. At the same time."

Leona sighed heavily, and then exploded a laugh. "You'll understand when you've been here long enough. Or at least you'll get used to it."

* * *

I sat side by side with Sarelli on the bridge, each with chin on knees and hands clasped around ankles, two cozy little bundles. In the yellow sunlight the river pulsed like the veins in an Ishian condor's wing membranes. I was feeling very good; and if part of that feeling was tomorrow morning with Doron, another part was this mellow afternoon with Sarelli. We'd finished my lesson early. Then we'd sauntered through Riverside to the bridge, picking up fallen leaves as we strolled, and dropped them two by two into the river, gleefully shouting our challenges to each other: "First in!" "Farthest out!" "Longest afloat!" "Soonest under!" Now we sat companionably quiet, talking off and on. I told him about shooting the rapids on three different worlds.

He sang a chuckle, chin to the sky. "Want to shoot the River Bimran?"

"Let's do it!" I rolled to my feet—or would have, if the gravity hadn't required boosting myself up with my arms. I was developing some interesting muscles. "Where can we get bubblesuits?"

Sarelli had no problem rolling to his feet and bouncing a little when he got there. "I keep a few for my students. It's a good concentration excercise, shooting the river."

"Why don't I ever see anybody doing it?"

He grinned. "Perhaps it's not as visible as you think?"

I looked down at the stone froth under the bridge, all arches and shadows and flashing glints. "Maybe not. But if there were very many of them, we'd see a few."

Sarelli's grin peaked. "The only ones we'd see here would be those who didn't get out in time. Upstream past the spaceport there's a wider stretch where the current isn't as vicious."

"So what are we waiting for?"

He snapped his fingers. "Shall we make a deal? You pick up something to eat, I'll pick up the bubblesuits, and we'll meet here in twenty minutes and take a floatcar."

"You trust me to get something you'll like?"

His eyebrows arched. "The least I can do, if you're willing to trust my bubblesuit."

I itched for that bubblesuit—any bubblesuit—and for that crazy river. I could feel the taut Bimran air sparkling in my lungs. *Tomorrow morning*, it sang. *Tomorrow morning.* I hoped the upstream site wouldn't be too placid.

The site was beautiful in the modest Bimran way. There was an island crystalline with birds, like a noisy white efflorescence. Between the glittering of the river and the rising and settling of the birds, the island seemed to jiggle in its place, and it took me a minute to realize that it was an island and not a giant raft.

The riverbank here was a narrow stretch of pebbly beach. We stood at the top of the steep-faced bluff that rose behind it, here and there draped by woody vines that arched out from the top and hung in dense green curtains to the pebbles. The opposite shore was wooded to the waterline, post-like trees with sheaves of thick foliage bristling from the nodes of their trunks.

Sarelli made a small sucking noise that I'd learned to recognize as a Bimranite sign of vexation. "Of course," he said, "there are other hazards besides currents."

A gaggle of tourists with their guide were hurrying down a steep path to occupy the upstream end of the beach. We contemplated them silently. If there was one thing a Bimranite and a starshipper could agree on without argument, this had to be it. "Why do you suppose they leave home?" I said. "They'd get more out of a good travelogue, and when they get back to their own world everything will have changed there."

Sarelli's nostrils widened. "Everyone needs scope. Some find their home world doesn't give them enough scope for arrogance. So they spread it around on Bimran."

The tour guide was handing out bubblesuits and the bolder tourists were putting them on. "Remember the beep!" the guide kept shouting. "Head for shore when you hear the beep. Stay away from the island—the birds are protected. Listen for the beep! Don't get in till I give the signal." He took one last scan of his flock with a hand-held counter and then loped downstream, past a scatter of picnickers and practicing stiltwalkers.

"What's he doing?" I asked Sarelli.

"What does it look like he's doing?"

"Looks like he's planting something on the bank downstream. Is that the beeper?"

"High probability it's a beacon to activate beepers in their suits when they pass it." Everything in Sarelli's face had taken on a disdainful curve. "Not relying on the beacon that's already there, which gives you an electrical tingle and doesn't require special equipment in the suit. Tourists seem to assume that a spontaneous, voluntary maintenance system can't work, and too many tour guides humor them."

The guide waved his arms and the suited tourists began plunging, wading, or crawling into the river. There was a strip of open water along the shore where little eddies ran downstream in procession. Some people stayed in that clear space, while others let themselves be whooshed into the labyrinth of arches and bubbles, disappearing and reappearing. Watching it from above was like watching a puppet show.

One of the picnickers downstream, a little woman in

brown with an intensely bright flower in her hand, walked up the bank toward the action. There's Bimran, I thought. She looked so typical—a little silly, maybe a little pitiful, but sweet; dressed in dullness and carrying a dazzling blue flower, watching the foreigners make fools of themselves.

"Race you down!" I challenged Sarelli, and we plunged down the slope, sliding and laughing, snatching at plants and rocks to keep some semblance of control over our descent.

"You win, Liss!"

"I had a head start. Let's go in."

The sound of the river here was softer and steadier, almost lost in the piping of the birds. I started to shed my loosesuit; you can get a bubblesuit on over most outfits, but this one was too bulky. I'd barely shrugged one shoulder out of its pink and green folds when Sarelli barked a laugh, not like his usual musical tinkle. "Another treat for the tourists, Rainbow Man? Shall I call them to attention?"

I stopped. It was true, the tourists still on the beach were all watching me. None of the tour group had taken off much clothing when they donned their own bubblesuits. A tourist contract generally includes agreeing not to shock either the natives or the other tourists. Probably bare skin was as out of bounds for this group as it was on Gantry Four. Probably some of these people were *from* Gantry Four, though the majority looked like Ishians. And while there were no rules about natives shocking tourists—natives or serious visitors— I'd been on Gantry Four myself, and there was something sickening about the looks you could get there just for having a visible body. I pulled the loosesuit over my shoulder again. "I'll be right back," I told Sarelli, and stepped through the curtain of hanging vines that jutted from the bluff's face.

It was like stepping into a resthall we'd had on the *Trojan*, where the direct lighting was all in sheets and narrow beams, and the walls more absorbent than reflective. Around me streaks of gentle yellow pierced the narrow openings between vines—slots in a filter of foliage. The ambient light was dim and greenish, and the pink stripes of my loosesuit showed almost gray.

Plenty of privacy, but not a very comfortable dressing room. Inside the outer foliage curtain there was a second, and I was sandwiched between them without space to lift an arm. I pushed through the inner curtain—the leaves here in the shade paler and broad as my hand—and walked into somebody else's privacy.

A few meters downstream, a man and a woman stood half among the trailing leafless stems of the next curtain in. They were so busy they didn't notice my rustles among the rustles of the breeze and the crying of the birds and the hum of the river. I stared at them a moment before I backed out, just as their heads started to turn my way.

Whatever transaction they were engaged in, it figured to be something that "wouldn't look right" to the eye of Bimran propriety. I didn't want to be involved with that. The man was obviously one of the tourists, the woman—when I thought it over—must have been the dull little person with the blue flower. What they were doing wouldn't have been so obvious if they hadn't tried to do it in the dark. The tourist had been pouring a long strand of currency into the woman's shoulder carry—high-denomination Ishian currency, the fluorescent kind.

Sarelli was balancing on one foot while he slipped the other into his bubblesuit. He greeted me with a mocking smile. "Too prickly for a starshipper?"

"Yes," I said. "Let's find another beach."

He made an acquiescent movement with his shoulders, whisked the filmy suit off his foot, and straightened up. A couple of meters downstream, vines swayed and the tourist emerged between them. "Good idea," Sarelli said too loudly. "I don't fancy sharing my river with Ishians."

The tourist shot him a hard look and strode down the beach away from us. "You can always tell them," Sarelli said. "Their faces look like the bottomside of a limpet."

Suddenly the whole scene had a bad taste, the golden afternoon as sour as spoiled mushfruit. I wadded the bubblesuit in my hands and thrust it at Sarelli. "Here," I said. "I'm going home."

He looked surprised for a moment—just till he could summon his trusty sneer. "Home, starshipper?" he said. "Where is that?"

Bottomside of a limpet, Sarelli had said. It's true that Ishians are uncannily pale. It's a bit of a shock at first sight. But pallor is a reflection of their history, not their character—and besides, a little ultraviolet radiation darkens them up to a nearly normal tone. They trace their genealogy to one of the old colony ships from Sirius Six, and the Sirian planets were colonized very early on, before there'd been any significant mixing of the old Earth populations. So Ishians represent an amazingly pure strain of one of the aboriginal varieties of the human species. "Caucasoid," they called themselves. I thought it was interesting.

I told myself the incident didn't matter. Sarelli had reasons for his prejudice. Ishians were notorious for being rude and aggressive, though I'd never had problems with them myself. It's normal, probably, to have some factual basis for your prejudices—just enough so you can say, "See, I told you so" every now and then. And other people's prejudices had never bothered me much before, even when they were against starshippers. Especially then.

Except that wasn't true. It was strangers' prejudices that didn't bother me. Strangers are easy to write off. You don't like me? Fine, that's your problem. You sort people by where they come from? Fine, I'll stay away from you. But Sarelli wasn't a stranger. I cared what he thought, because I liked him. And when Sarelli said, *I don't like Ishians,* what I heard was, *If you were an Ishian, I wouldn't like you.* And I might have been an Ishian. I might have been anything. If he was prejudiced against anybody, he was prejudiced against me.

≈ 7 ≈

Whether working on a case or between cases, Selectors are encouraged to notice possible future candidates for Selection and to make preliminary notes on their behavior. A Selector who is not observant at all times is not a good Selector.

—*From* Revised Manual for Selectors,
Working Draft, Chapter 1.

I got to the Park early, but Doron was waiting for me, just opposite the little drinkshop where we'd talked. He was already coming toward me when I spotted him. We didn't speak until we both stopped, less than a meter apart.

"Nice day, Liss." His eyes twinkled. Eyes don't actually twinkle. It's the effect of the little lines at the corners, the little movements of cheeks and eyelids. Eyes don't twinkle so much in free-fall.

A wonderful laziness came over me. I didn't want to shoot any rapids today. I felt heavy and warm, in spite of the chill morning air. "Where shall we go?" I asked him.

"We could visit some of the hot springs," Doron said. "Or the mineral lake."

Hot springs were rare in the Gemmeus Cluster, which was why every world blessed with some of them showed them off persistently to visitors. "How about the mineral lake?" I said.

He hesitated just an instant. "If you like." A tone of absolutely excessive moderation.

I laughed. "Well, it was your suggestion, Doron."

"Oh, yes," he said soberly. "It's something everyone should see."

We took a tunneltrain, which was faster and more expensive than any other way to get there. Bimran wasn't a small planet, but the population was tiny, scattered along the temperate river valleys of the only serious continent. Bimran City was the one real urban settlement, and on some worlds it would have been classed as a village. Elsewhere there were small farms, real villages, and the sights that people went to see. Those, Doron told me, were all connected to Bimran City by tunneltrains.

He insisted on paying my fare. "Selectors travel a lot," he said. "And usually my transportation is paid for. It's not often I get to do the same for anyone else."

I accepted cheerfully. I'd be here for a long time, and my capital wasn't infinite. I didn't want to have to actually work for a living.

The tunneltrain was a single plump snake of a perfectly normal elastic, proving that Leona was right: Bimranites could have had things softer if they'd wanted to. "The tunnel has a great many curves," Doron explained—apologizing for the lack of rigidity. "It's because of the geological structure."

"That's fine," I said, seesawing my weight on the yielding floor. "I like it."

"Do you? It makes many people uneasy. Some won't ride the trains at all."

Maybe so, but there were plenty of passengers on this one. It was fifty or sixty meters long and a good four wide, with aisles down both sides and a forest of mushrooms in the middle, most of them occupied.

"Flowers," Doron corrected me. "Not mushrooms. See

the petals." We sat down near one end of the train, and the petals of our flowers closed around us. "It's for safety," Doron explained, tucking the corner of a petal under his arm. "But even this makes some people feel insecure. It's interesting how different individuals react to what's externally the same stimulus."

A tone sounded, the door whooshed shut, the few empty flowers flapped their petals forlornly, and the train began to move with a definite jerk. After that, though, it settled down, and there was no way to tell we were traveling except the changing shape of the chamber as the snake writhed its way through the tunnel. There were the typical Bimran crowd noises—a hum of small talk punctuated by cries of delight as walls bent or floor arched for a curve.

"Of course," Doron said, "if it were really the same stimulus, it would get the same response. Humans are very uniform in their responses."

"Are they?" I said. "Then why do they act so different?"

"Because they're receiving different stimuli," Doron said. "You might look at that man in brown."

"Which one?"

"A little to the left—five rows ahead—the frightened one. You see?"

I didn't at first. It wasn't until the particular man in brown laughed too loudly that I focused on him. Then I noticed the way he kept fingering the petal that enfolded his chest, and the tension of his other hand on his knees, and the restless looks he threw from one wall to the other. "All right, so he's scared. Why is he scared and we're not?"

"Because he's getting different stimuli. Look, there's another one. Farther forward on the right—that woman in gray—you see?"

"Ye-es," I said doubtfully. "You're better at this than I

am. Why different stimuli? We're all in the same capsule."

"That means we get more or less the same external input," Doron said. "But not the same effective stimuli—not the stimuli that trigger our physical and emotional responses."

"Why not?"

"Because the input is filtered and directed by very different layers of memory, very different biochemical and bioelectric interfaces."

"And a good thing, too," I said. "You could get a really monotonous universe otherwise."

"Do you think so?" A funny thing to sound wistful about.

I tilted my head to look at him slantwise. He looked just as good. "All identical stimuli and all identical responses? Yes, I think so!"

"But look at the universe," Doron said. The train bent suddenly; a sharp angle ran along both walls, crowding my flower briefly close to Doron's, and left us straight and separate again. "Look at Bimran. This is a comparatively happy planet. No war, no government oppression, no famines, no plagues, no overpopulation. But there are people in misery right now on Bimran—hundreds, thousands of people." He was hurting again; I saw him hurt. I thought of all the worlds I'd seen, all the pains that had died. "I don't mean just deliberate cruelties," Doron said, "though at first glance that seems the most horrible thing. I mean the accidental evils, the unintentional abuses people inflict on each other simply because they don't realize what stimuli they're administering. And the calamities that seem to be beyond human control, or at least individual control." He had twisted his flower to face me straight with his hurt eyes. "What kind of God," he asked me, "would allow all these things?"

"I thought you were in favor of God," I said.

He smiled his sweet smile, but the eyes still ached. "Anybody who's in favor of God, as you put it, has got to face these things. It's cowardice not to."

"So what's the answer? What kind of God would allow these things?"

"A just God," he said. "There's no other possibility."

The train gave its little jerk, a tone sounded, the door opened behind us. "Here we are," Doron said cheerfully.

The Mineral Lake—that was its name—lay in the middle of a steep-sided valley. We came up out of the tunnel in the crowd of passengers and walked across a stretch of flatness littered with sand. The sun was high now, and the sky burned. "It's almost hot," I said.

Doron beamed, as if the warmth were something he'd arranged specially to surprise me. "It's always warmer here," he said. "That's why it's so popular."

That might have been one reason, but I was staring bewildered at another. A low bench, no more than ankle height, ran along the lakeshore a few meters from the water, and as people reached it they stepped over, methodically took off their clothes, laid them on the bench, and trotted naked down the beach. I looked at Doron. He was walking with his eyes aimed steadfastly forward. "I don't know how you feel about nudity," he said.

"I'm all for it, when appropriate." I stepped over the bench.

"I know it's taboo in some cultures," Doron said.

"I don't have taboos," I said, and began to pull off my walkingsuit. He stepped over the bench beside me.

He was utterly huggable. He wasn't used to being naked, obviously—the shy boy with nothing left to hide behind—but Doron couldn't have been awkward if he tried. I was disappointed to see only the mildest preliminary stirrings of an erection; but when he straightened up from laying his clothes on the bench and found my eyes on him, it suddenly swiveled into launch position. I looked firmly at his face, which was also adorable. A flush showed on his cheekbones, where his beard thinned out, and he smiled such a smile— sweet, dignified, apologetic all at once—that I could have forgiven him anything. "Let's go in," he said. His erection was already collapsing. Penis control, I thought, would be one of the things Sarelli taught to qualified students.

Definitely this was still Bimran. Everybody was bare, but nobody was touching anybody. Doron and I weren't the only couple separated by about the length of a forearm. We waded in. The water was as warm as the air, and when you shoved it, it shoved back. Trying to wade that water was almost like walking on Old Kossolo, where the gravity shortens you by about two inches on your first step. I did what I saw other people doing—threw myself forward onto the lake as if it were a trampoline. Doron dropped beside me with a bounce and a splash, and we floated laughing, almost nose to nose. He oared himself forward with his hands—it was too shallow and too dense for proper swimming—and I kept up with him as well as I could, adding my own contributions to the wet uproar of laughter and splashing and yells around us. We didn't stop until we'd found our own vacant piece of lake, well out from shore and well past the aquatic crowds.

"How deep is it here?" I asked him.

He blushed outright. "I don't know."

I couldn't help laughing. When sex reared its pretty head, he had kept his embarrassment down to a glow on the cheekbones; but admitting ignorance about a tourist attraction made his whole face flame. It was a rich color, like the deep-toned tangberry wines of Ishi Three, and I wanted to warm my fingers on it.

"Nothing sinks," Doron added. "That's because of the dissolved minerals. I suppose I never thought about the depth." He was getting his color under control again. I should feel very flattered to have inspired that first spontaneous response beside the bench.

"I don't really want to know about the depth," I said. The water moved under me, rolling and rolling in a gentle swell. "I'm more curious about the people on the surface. I never expected to see a Bimran crowd floating around without clothes."

"Didn't you?" he said mildly. "Why not?"

I rolled over onto my back—not as easy as it sounds—and laughed up at the dazzling sky. There it was again, the starshipper's fallacy, the thing we always warn each other against. *When you see a tail, don't assume there's a rat at the end of it.* You're always tempted to build too much on the familiar-looking bits of an unknown culture. "The Bimranites I've seen before today," I said cautiously, "always seemed careful not to call attention to their bodies."

"Exactly," Doron said. I draped my arm across my eyes to cut the glare. I could tell without looking that he was smiling at me. "And nothing calls more attention to bodies than keeping them hidden. There have been cultures where the human body itself was identified with sexual activity."

"Yes," I said. "There still are some. Or were when I was there." Up, down, up, down, the gentle massage of the lake cradled my backside. It was lovely to float undulating there, the next best thing to bonelessness, the water lifting and lowering legs, hips, chests, shoulders, heads in turn.

"And in those cultures," Doron went on, "people can become so habituated to thinking in sexual terms that any unveiling of the body is assumed to have a sexual intention."

"Yes, I know. If you show a spot of skin, people take it as

an invitation. Gantry Four was like that." I shuddered in the warm water. From Gantry to Bimran seemed to be from one extreme to another. Sometimes you can't help wondering if the only moderates in the universe are starshippers.

"That's why," Doron said, "we think it's important not to have any kind of nudity taboo. I should say that's *one* of the reasons."

I looked at him from under my elbow. He was still floating on his stomach, his cheek on one bent arm. "What's another reason?"

Every time he spoke, I could detect a tightening and loosening in his neat little buttocks, the wink of a dimple like a visible echo. He was more muscular than I'd expected, his whole slim body laced with the visible tools of strength. "Naturally," he said, in that student's voice of his, "there may be sexual arousal when people see each other undressed."

"Naturally." I couldn't have agreed more.

"So we think it's important for people to be familiar with that phenomenon and not to see it as a sign of lust—no more than salivation at the sight of food is a sign of gluttony. And just as important for them to learn to control it."

"I see," I said lazily. The happy yelps of Bimranites controlling their phenomena made distant background music. Between the baking air and the caressing water, I could have been embalmed alive and never noticed it. I closed my eyes. "What does a Selector do when he isn't floating?" I asked.

He didn't answer for so long that I opened my eyes again. He had changed position, facing me almost on his side, sculling with one hand to keep himself balanced in the water. "I'm sorry," he said. "I want to tell you, but I'm not sure where to begin."

"Begin with Doron," I said.

"No. I think it's necessary to begin with God. God is just."

That was what he'd said on the train, and I remembered the context uneasily. "What makes you so sure this God of yours is a just one?"

"We know that God cares for the created universe, and specifically for humans. We know—"

"How?"

He paused, puzzled. "How does God care?"

"How do you know?"

"Oh, I see. We know from the revelations humans have received—the very fact of revelations. And prayers answered, and all the benign aspects of the universe. It adds up to a virtual certainty."

"Mmm." I was floating in a benign aspect, easy as free-fall but all heavy, heavy and warm. Womb pressure. "Caring equals justice?"

"No, no," he said. "Not in itself. But we also know that God demands justice of us."

"Revelation?"

"Yes, revelation. And we know that God is all-knowing and all-powerful."

"Revelation?"

He laughed. "Axiom. Omniscience and omnipotence are basic characteristics of God, part of the definition. Believing in God at all means acknowledging them."

"Mmmm," I said. Buoyancy, that was the word. Bobbing in an ocean of warmth.

"Do you see?" Doron urged gently. "God is capable of relieving all suffering. God cares about us. And yet we suffer. It must be because we deserve suffering."

I lifted my arm to look at him. "What?" I wasn't sure I'd heard it right. The sun and the water were deactivating my brain.

"Given an omnipotent and caring Deity, it follows that all the suffering in the universe is acceptable," Doron said. "Nothing can exist without God's acceptance. More than that; since God cares for us, nothing can happen that is not for our good."

"Who's 'us'?"

He gazed at me, not just from the neck up. "You and me," he said. "Bimranites. Starshippers. Human beings."

"Selectors?"

"Yes, Selectors. In a sense we're all Selectors. What makes a human being human is the ability to select—to choose between good and bad."

"I thought you said everything was good."

"Oh, no." He looked distressed. "What did I say to make you think that?"

"Something about everything being all right with God."

"Oh, I see." His face cleared a little. "I didn't express it very well. Everything that exists, everything that happens, is acceptable to God in the sense that God allows it to exist or to happen. That doesn't mean that everything is equally desirable, or equally pleasing to God. We've been given Commandments to follow—I've told you about that. What Selectors do—" a stronger swell of the lake lifted his shoulders "—is to identify people who have kept the Commandments well, and people who have broken them."

It wasn't just warm, I decided, it was really too hot—laid flat on that impenetrable bed of water, with no wisp of shadow between me and that burning sky, sandwiched between wet heat and dry heat, nothing of me untouched. I splashed my arms restlessly. "And what do you do with those people?"

"I take them to Bliss or to Punishment," he said.

"What's Bliss? What's Punishment?" I didn't know why I sounded so angry. He'd tossed those words at me before.

He paused again—looking for the way to tell me. "Appropriate stimuli," he said at last. "They receive appropriate stimuli for the rest of their lives. And they are kept alive as long as possible."

"Bimran version of heaven and hell," I said, getting it as straight as I could. It's not easy to get things straight when you're bobbing like a morsel in somebody's soup.

"Yes, in a way," Doron said. "I suppose this must sound silly to you, Liss—"

"Horrible," I said. "Horrible is how it sounds."

He looked wounded. Not just his eyes but his whole beautiful body seemed to shrink away from me, or from what I was thinking. "We know our limitations," he said. "We don't risk making mistakes; it's too serious. Only a few people are Selected—only the extreme cases. Does that make it less horrible to you?"

"I don't know. How does it feel to be a Selector?"

"We're trained for it," he said. "Intensively trained. And we have a *Manual*. It's very helpful, the *Manual*. Invaluable." He broke off and started again. "Liss—"

He was hurting, he was pleading. "What?" I said.

"I'm a human being." He smiled a small, shy smile. "It's every human's duty to relieve suffering and to prevent suffering wherever possible. Selectors are not exempt."

≈ **8** ≈

It is the duty of every individual to relieve suffering wherever found and to prevent it wherever possible. It is the duty of society to inflict suffering where deserved.
—*From* Revised Manual for Selectors,
Working Draft, Introduction.

When I was on Minos, the biggest building in every community (they didn't have cities on Minos) was the temple. Groups of people gathered there every day for short worship services, and once a month the whole community poured in for a major ceremony that lasted hours and involved everybody present in a dense weave of sound and colors and motion. There was a considerable body of clergy, very hierarchized, the lower orders chosen by lot from the community population, the higher ones elected or co-opted, all the way up to the Council of Prophets that took their orders direct from the local deity. (That's "local" in a starshipper's sense. Like Bimranites, Miniotes recognized only one god. Unlike Bimranites, they didn't make it responsible for the whole universe.)

That was religion I could understand. People got a lot of emotional and social and aesthetic satisfaction out of it. There were wonderful careers for the talented and the enterprising, solace and help for the unlucky, and a sense of belonging for everybody, not to mention the entertainment.

And then on Paradiso the *Trojan* had run up against what I would call a real theocracy. We all had to be fumigated before we were allowed to leave the spaceport, to get rid of every speck of alien divinities we might be carrying. There were plenty of local divinities, including the assorted autocrats and oligarchs who ran things in various cities, islands, and subterranea, and of course the super-autocrat who ostensibly ran the whole planet. Failure to perform the proper rituals before the holy form of any of these dinky deities was an actionable offense. There were dissidents all over the place, who seemed generally to express their dissidence by producing new gods, or latching onto lesser members of the official pantheon and giving them a protest theology. The *Trojan* got into trouble when we traded a load of aluminum for gold and found out afterwards that aluminum was a controlled commodity and we'd been dealing with a dissident group. I personally just missed being taken hostage, and we had to do a lot of dickering, payoffs, and salaaming to local divinities before we were able to leave with our crew intact.

But on Bimran, religion was invisible, like a gravitational field holding people in their orbits. Holding me too, whether I liked it or not. My orbit now was meeting Doron every morning, visiting the day's attraction, and getting back to Bimran City no later than nightfall, often by noon. Anything longer, I supposed, wouldn't look right.

We saw other naked places besides the Mineral Lake— hot springs, mostly. Offworld tours visited a few of them, to see Bimranite skin exposed to unmediated nature. If any of the tourists hoped to see Bimranite orgies, they were certainly disappointed. Bimranites bare were as prim as Bimranites clothed—more so, if anything. And it was always all or none; at any given resort, you found everybody naked or everybody dressed. The more I saw of Bimranites, the more I appreciated Sarelli's nonconformity. He moved in a standard orbit, but with his own speed and spin. Never mind his boorishness with the Ishian at the river; I liked the way he struck sparks from everything he touched. He was comfortable to be with in the same way Bimranite air was comfortable to breathe—a little extra pressure, a little extra tang.

"What do you have against Ishians, Sarelli?" It was our first lesson day after the aborted rivershoot, and I'd waited till the lesson was over to put it to him.

"What do you suppose?"

"I'm not supposing. I had a wonderful time in the Ishian system."

"Bravo, Rainbow Man! Not many people achieve that."

"Maybe it's easier for starshippers. We learn early on that every world has its own style."

He flashed a grin. "Exactly."

"So what do you have against Ishians? It's your turn to answer a question."

"Is it?"

"Yes. I told you my favorite flavor of munchcakes."

"Fair enough." He tossed one of the little cakes into the air and caught it. "I don't like what passes for morality in Ishian societies. And I've heard too many stories about their arrogance and selfishness. Not a style that appeals to me." He popped the munchcake into his mouth and crunched it while he tossed three to me in quick succession. "I talked to a tourist from Gantry Four who was three years late getting home because his Ishian host didn't wake him in time to catch his shuttle. That's one example. I've seen Ishians bump people off a path without apologizing. I've heard them accuse honest shopkeepers of cheating them—"

"And I've seen Ishians drop everything to help each other, I've seen them deliberately lose money on a deal to avoid hurting someone's feelings, I've seen them stooping in the mud to help a child who fell down—Sarelli, you can't condemn them all because you don't like what some of them have done."

"I don't condemn them all. I condemn the majority of them. I'm quite willing to be delighted by exceptions."

"But you do condemn them all. You expect every one of them you meet to fit your picture of the nasty Ishian, and the burden is on the Ishian to convince you otherwise."

"I expect any given Ishian to be part of the Ishian majority. Chances favor the accuracy of that prediction."

"I thought you were broad-minded, Sarelli."

He crunched a munchcake. "I am broad-minded. Very broad-minded. You should know, Rainbow Man."

But I was learning the boundaries of Sarelli's broad-mindedness. By way of experiment I invited him to come with me to one of the places I'd been with Doron—the hot springs of Pels, where the sport was to lie naked in the snow of a deep ravine and then throw yourself into the steaming water. He was too busy, he said; and besides, the snow was no good this late in the summer. I proposed another try at shooting the rapids. He was always too busy.

I didn't doubt that at least some of that busyness was real. A lot of the work that got done on Bimran was what they called "voluntary labor" (which in some places I've known would have been an oxymoron). On a purely private scale, people rallied round to help a friend build new quarters, find a job, or care for an incapacitated neighbor or relative. What on many worlds would have been public properties and public services—like streets, or the floatcars that drifted along them, paying minuscule tolls at every major intersection—were private commercial enterprises here; but they were heavily subsidized by the voluntary labor of their users and anyone else who felt the urge to pitch in. Other things (most schools, I gathered, as well as parks and public buildings like the museum) were entirely the work of informal cooperatives with no very definite membership—the kind of "spontaneous maintenance" that Sarelli had talked about. Somehow it all worked pretty well.

Leona helped me understand. She had gone local to the extent of participating in some of these public-spirited pastimes. When she wasn't chatting with the landlord or a passerby, she was likely to be delivering hot meals and gossip to shut-ins, or weeding flowerbeds in the Park. "It's something to do," she said, "and it helps keep things running. When things don't run right, people get irritable, and the whole planet gets a little less comfortable to live on. Of course, I don't have as much motivation as a Bimranite does."

"Why not?" I asked. "You live on the planet just as much as they do."

She laughed. "Maybe so, but I can get off it if I want to. And I'm not eligible for Selection. They're piling up good behavior points. Take care of your fellow Bimranites and you'll end up in Bliss—or at least you won't end up in Punishment. That's the idea."

"Is somebody keeping score?" It looked too disorganized for that.

"No, but people notice. When Selectors get interested in somebody, they do a lot of watching . . . and listening

. . . and talking to everybody who's ever known the person."

This was more about the Selection process than I'd ever learned from Doron. "So how do Selectors get interested in somebody?"

"Well, nobody knows exactly. They're pretty close-mouthed about their procedures. They do a lot of random scanning, for sure—actually it's not for sure, but it looks that way. And they probably just home in on anybody who looks good. Or bad."

I looped back my sleeves and squatted beside her. "Is this a weed?"

"Yes, all these scraggly-looking things with the floppy branches. You have to trace them back to the main stem and get hold of it right at ground level."

I traced, gripped, and tugged, and the root came loose so unexpectedly that I ended up flat on my bottom in the dirt. "Oops!"

Leona, solidly planted on her knees, emitted a cordial bellow of laughter. "Sorry. Should have warned you."

"Hazards of going local," I said, and righted myself. "I don't think you give Bimranites enough credit. There's more to Bimran than Selection."

"Thank the gods, yes!" She chuckled. "But we might as well face it, Liss; what keeps Bimranite society sweet and simple—the way you and I like it—is knowing there's a Selector looking over everybody's shoulder."

"You're a cynic, Leona! I think most Bimranites try to be good people because they *are* sweet and simple. I don't think it takes Selection to keep them that way."

"Talking about individuals, you're right," she said. "Talking about the society, I'm right. Come on, Liss, I know you've seen worlds where the typical Bimranite wouldn't survive three days without a major change of policy. It's

Bimran society that gives Bimranites the option of being lovable."

"Then I say, Three cheers for Bimran society! Look, is this a weed?"

She peered. "Yes, but that's a tough one. Wait till somebody comes with a vibrator to loosen up the soil." She chuckled. "You'll get the hang of it, Liss. It just takes a while."

I wasn't getting the hang of it fast enough; that was the bleak truth, and a truth I hadn't been prepared for when I left the *Trojan*. Pulling weeds with Leona, arguing with Sarelli, I could be cheerful and easy. But alone in my sleep-swing, waiting for consciousness to deactivate and give me a rest, I felt all the sore places where Bimran and I were rubbing each other the wrong way. Sarelli and the Ishian . . . Sarelli and his meaningful sneers . . . the sexlessness of life for the Rainbow Man . . . and the sorest, tenderest spot of all: gentle Doron as Selector for Bliss and Punishment.

Whatever else (I told myself gravely) he was doing me a genuine useful service by showing me around Bimran. On that excuse, I headed morning after morning for the Park, though half the time Doron met me on the way. And in the bright Bimran air, the warm colors of Bimran sunlight, I forgot about the nights every time.

We would eat together in some restaurant, or buy portable food and eat it in one of the small neighborhood parks or while we strolled. After a bit we'd find a floatcar or walk to the tunneltrain station at the east edge of Southtown, and begin our day's expedition.

But a planet's night is always there, just around the curve, waiting for you to roll into it. I was already feeling it, and restless with it, and feeling that Doron was restless too, the morning he said out of a brief silence, "I won't be able to take you to the glacier today. I'm sorry."

"Oh, I'm sorry too. Tomorrow, then?"

He looked melancholy. "Perhaps in a few weeks, or—perhaps not. I've been assigned to a case."

We'd done more strolling than usual that morning, across the river to wander up the west bank—putting this off, I realized now. We were on the way back toward my part of town, crossing the same bridge where I'd sat with Sarelli, hearing the same river noises. The wind shoved at us, billowing my yellow cloak till its translucent folds plastered themselves against Doron's black-clad arm and chest. "Assigned to a case," I said. I didn't know if it was just disappointment I felt, or something more. "Does that mean you'll be passing judgment on somebody?"

"No. It means I'll be observing someone and preparing a report."

"Then who makes the judgment?"

"The system makes it. Once the report is prepared, the judgment is automatic. That's why," he added, "it's important for my report to be perfectly accurate."

"In other words," I said restively, "you make the judgment." A gust of wind pushed me against him. I felt his hand on my arm for a moment, firm through the folds of cloak, as we straightened ourselves.

"In effect, yes," he said. "Yes," he said again.

This bridge was hazardous, I thought. Bimranites might be prim and cautious, but they didn't put up a simple barrier to keep you from getting blown into the river. "And I suppose," I said, "that means you check up on everything somebody has ever done." My cloak billowed out again, shrouding my view of him in yellow, and I pulled it back and tucked it tight around myself. "I suppose you've got a checklist of about fifty thousand things they're not allowed to do, like holding hands in public—"

He stood still, and I stopped to face him. "It's not like that," he said, dismayed. "The only rules that people have to follow are the Commandments."

"And how many commandments are there?"

"Four."

"Four? You're joking, Doron."

"Exactly four."

The wind eased for a moment. I readjusted my cloak, thinking about what he'd just said. "So you simply check on whether somebody has followed four rules?"

He smiled a little wryly. "The Commandments are simple. Judging how well an individual has applied them can be very complex. That's why—" I saw his face tighten briefly. "I brought something for you, Liss. Not a gift; it can only be a loan. But you can keep it as long as you like. On one condition." His face was suddenly as naked as his body had been at the Mineral Lake or in the melting snow at Pels. Nothing to hide behind.

"What condition?"

"That you keep it entirely private. Not to speak of it, not to let anyone know you have it."

A gust of wind pushed me closer, and he didn't back away. "Entirely private," I said. "Yes, I agree to that."

My cloak billowed again, joining or separating us with a yellow cloud, veiling Doron's face for a moment. "Here it is," he said. Something touched my hand through the folds. I pulled the cloak back under control and accepted what he was holding out to me. An ordinary Bimran book—just a little flat black box, contoured for the hand, with inset pressure points for visual and aural access. I turned it over. No socket for copying. No visible title.

"Is this your *Manual?*"

He made a little gesture with his hand, and I pocketed the book quickly. Wouldn't look right, would it? And this was more than an ordinary matter of Bimran propriety, I could tell that much. "Yes, it's the *Manual,*" he said. "My own copy."

We walked on. Something had eased between us. I knew the feeling. Decision taken and applied—it felt good, and never mind the consequences. I'd felt that way when I stepped out of the *Trojan*'s lander for the last time. "Most of it's quite technical and dry," Doron said. "I don't suppose you'll want to read it all. It's only a working draft. The whole Selection system is still under development. The *Manual* is barely a hundred years old, and we're already working on the third revision."

I smiled. "Sounds pretty stable to me. What did you do before the *Manual?*"

"It was a very unhappy time," he said. We reached the end of the bridge and turned down the street that would lead us to my quarters. The wind was in our faces.

"What happened?" I asked.

"Bimran almost failed," Doron said. He sounded desolate, as if it had been his own almost-failure. "The founders meant this to be a planet where everyone is free to live without the pressures that drive people away from God's Commandments—or suck people away from them. No law but God's law, no government, no church, no organization except a migration control system to keep the original purpose from being drowned in a flood of contrary intentions."

"And it didn't work?" I asked sympathetically. Bimran wasn't the only world that had tried to isolate itself from alien ideas. But even demolishing spaceports doesn't keep out the universe forever.

"Oh, it worked very well," he said. "But not perfectly. In the course of a few centuries, abuses built up to such a level that Bimran wasn't much better than many other worlds."

"Terrible," I said.

His eyes twinkled. Yes, they did. I could have put up my hand and caught particle showers of little sparks. "You always laugh at me, Liss—very rightly. But can you understand?"

"Yes, I think I do understand. I wouldn't want to see Bimran spoiled, either."

"That was when the Selection Corps was founded—a small group of volunteers who wanted to help Bimran get back into orbit."

"Vigilantes," I said.

"I suppose you could say so. But Selection would never have worked if it hadn't been popular. It's not something that was imposed on Bimranites, Liss; it's something Bimranites wanted and welcomed. Can you understand?"

I laughed aloud. "I can understand, Doron, I can understand everything. When can I see you?"

And his face was veiled again, more veiled by his thoughts than it had been by my cloak. "I don't know," he said.

≈ 9 ≈

On a psychological level, the Commandments may be summarized by a single rule: Do nothing you know to be harmful. *This, of course, presupposes knowledge.*
— *From* Revised Manual for Selectors,
Working Draft, Conclusions.

Don't you ever worship your God?" I asked Sarelli.

His laughter flowed. "Don't you ever sleep, Rainbow Man?"

"Is that an answer?"

"Is that a question?" He handed me a slice of waxfruit, his fingers sliding along it as if they couldn't quite break the connection.

I stroked the slice myself—waxfruit *was* smooth, really better to play with than to eat—and nibbled one end. "You mean you don't do your worshiping in public."

"Exactly right. What goes on between me and God is no one else's business."

It was a little hard for me to picture anything going on between Sarelli and God. But then, it was a little hard for me to picture God. "Don't let me intrude," I said.

"Did you think I would?" Sharp-edged Sarelli. You had to get past the glitter to touch the warmth. "Public worship," he said, "is something people do to impress each other. The carnival stage of religious development."

"Is that bad?"

He lifted his eyebrows. "It doesn't do anything for God."

"And what do you do for God?"

He smiled sweetly. "Keep the Commandments."

"Sarelli—" I sucked the waxfruit. It was like sucking wax.

"What is it, pretty Liss?"

"If your Commandments tell you to do smart things, then you don't need Commandments, you could figure it out on your own. If your Commandments tell you to do stupid things, then you shouldn't keep them."

He didn't burst into laughter, as I'd expected. He smiled gently. "No, no, Rainbow Man. You have it quite reversed. It so happens that the Commandments are reasonable. But that's God's business, not ours. In a sense it doesn't matter what the Commandments are. They could be perfectly arbitrary. They could seem completely trivial to human reason. Do you know what the only important thing about a commandment is?"

"Tell me."

And now he laughed, gloriously, brilliantly. "A commandment," he said, "must be obeyed."

I missed Doron. More than once I took out his *Manual,* stroking and fingering it, thinking about where he might have carried it, what parts of his body it might have nestled close to. One of these days I would have to read some of it, if only to tell him that I had. The trouble was, I didn't exactly feel eager to know the technical details of what he was doing. I only wished I had some idea of how long his case might last. But he didn't know that himself; the *Manual* certainly wouldn't tell me.

In the meantime, I had considerable fun with Sarelli. We would start with a leisurely sundown meal in some restaurant, watching other diners arrive and eat and go their ways while we dawdled, and then we would begin to roam. I liked Bimran after dark; I liked the night sky. It wasn't the overwhelming dazzle you get in the heart of the cluster, but real night with real stars, and the white cloud of a real Milky Way trailing slantwise off behind them, and sometimes a moon, just big enough to show its disk but bright as a beacon. Atmospheric clouds, too, complicating the patterns of the sky, so it was never the same on two nights running. But on a clear night—the moon aside—it wasn't much different from what you'd expect from a starship viewport when you're entering docking orbit, after the slud has kicked off and gravitation has gentled you down to a sweet, slow drift. It gave me a feeling of being still tuned in to reality. Bimran City was a badly underlit town by most standards, and except in a few spots its buildings were low, which meant neither city glow nor architectural obstruction to interfere with sky-watching. And once I'd bought my own footboard, Sarelli and I did a lot of cruising.

"Do you want to hear Vailid?" Sarelli asked me, with that something-held-back grin he did so well.

"Who's Vailid?"

He looked surprised, maybe genuinely so. "You haven't heard of Vailid?"

I laughed at him. "No, I haven't heard of Vailid. Tell me about Vailid."

"Oh, well, another myth exploded. Offworlders don't all belong to one giant subversive network, after all."

"Oh, slud! I thought Vailid would be a native phenomenon. I can see offworlders offworld."

He grinned wider. *"Hear* is the thing, I understand."

"Oh, in that case—" Bimranite music was all right, but I could cheerfully take a change.

"Here we go, then," Sarelli said, and spun his footboard, a mobile glisten in the starlight. One thing I liked about Sarelli was the way he was always ready to veer, to reverse course, to spin his footboard and wheel off in the opposite direction for a bit of fun. You can't do that with a starship.

Farther from the Park there was even less light, and the streets were even more confusing. You couldn't really get lost in Bimran City. It wasn't big enough, and the river gave you an unchanging arrow of direction. But maybe that was exactly why the street plan was so irregular; Bimranites couldn't get lost in their city, but they could get pleasantly bewildered.

We were somewhere in the depths of Southtown, far past my neighborhood, when Sarelli slowed. I swerved around him, and heard his laugh in the dark. "Just on your right," he said. "I'll see you tomorrow, perhaps."

"What?" But he must have pressed his heel hard on the accelerator, and there I was alone beside a glimmer of light. Blue light.

It was a luminous curtain in a doorway. I pushed it aside and was looking into a small cube of a room, dimly lit with the same blue. "Please come in," a soft artificial voice invited me. "Please put on a cloak before you enter the meeting room."

I saw a stack of what looked like folded cloth in one corner, multiple shades of blue in the blueness, and a disorderly heap of footboards sprawling against the opposite wall. I picked up my own board and stepped in, letting the curtain close behind me. "Please put on a cloak before you enter the meeting room," the voice repeated softly. Another luminous blue curtain in the back wall marked what was presumably the meeting room entrance.

I added my footboard to the pile, at the edge nearest the

outer curtain, and picked up the top cloth from the blue
stack. Fold upon fold followed, and for a moment I thought
the whole stack was one voluminous strip. But no, what I
held was only a couple of meters of soft, heavy fabric. I
draped it around myself, totally eclipsing the burnt orange
and slick white of my sleeksuit, and eased quietly through the
meeting room doorway, stirring the curtain as little as possible.

Inside, the lighting was all white, a little cooler than Bimran normal, but almost everything else was blue. The exception was the flat white squares laid in order on the
blue-draped table—sheets of blank white paper, one in front
of each person who sat there. In the crisp white light the
contrast was stark. I glanced back at my exit. The blue
curtain of the doorway (not luminous on this side) was a
cascade of striped and mingling darkness and pallor, blues
blending into blues. Around the table, faces looked up at me,
some with bright smiles, some with the defensive expressions
of people who aren't sure they want to be seen where they
are. Somebody sprang up smoothly to meet me, holding one
hand in front of her mouth as a request for silence, and led
me to a cushion beside the table. I sat down, and she settled
on her own cushion beside me.

It was very still. I counted seventeen people around the
table besides myself, all wrapped in different shades of blue,
pale or deep but all cool and smooth as a Bimran waterfall.
Nobody spoke. Some watched me curiously, or suspiciously,
or blankly. Some sat with eyes closed or half-closed. Some
exchanged glances or contemplative stares with their neighbors. I tried smiling, which got a few mild flickers of response
and several averted gazes.

With a hiss, a panel of pale blue wall opened on darkness,
and a figure stepped into the room. We all shifted on our

cushions for a better view. The panel closed, and the new-comer stood out stark against the pallor of the wall, hooded and robed in a glistening midnight blue. The beardless face could have been a man's or a woman's—even without the complications of Bimran terminology—and so could the clear, astringent voice. "My parents escaped from Bimran sixty-three years ago. I have returned, to make Bimran free."

I hoped it was true about there being no police on Bimran. I could see myself trying to explain: "Honestly, officer, I thought I was going to hear a concert of offworld music; I had no idea it was a subversive organization." One thing for certain, this was the last time I'd let Sarelli steer me into an unmarked doorway and take off like a starship.

Vailid (this had to be Vailid) moved forward smoothly, sank to a vacant cushion, and raised slim hands to push back the lustrous hood. Woman, I decided—genetically speaking, at least. Not extremely young, not extremely old. Her eyes—long, narrow, and dark, like her fingers—came straight to mine. "There are new listeners among us tonight," she said. "The word is spreading." I heard an approving murmur from some of the people around the table. "We are not here—" she was speaking directly to me, and I didn't think it was just because I happened to be sitting opposite her— "to conspire. We are here to commune. We are here to change the world by loving it."

I relaxed a few degrees. On another planet, that would have meant I was in for a dose of religion, not subversion. But what would subversion mean on Bimran? There was no government to overthrow; there was only Selection. Still, these people weren't hiding out—or not doing it very well.

Vailid lifted one arm, trailing a curtain of midnight drapery, and let it fall again. Scene One, I thought. "Most of you know," she said, "that I am Bimran-born. Most of you know that I left Bimran." Her voice rose suddenly, with a passion-ate quiver. "Yes, left Bimran. Escaped from Bimran! My parents' love, their courage, their good fortune—and good fortune, friends, is not a matter of chance—would not per-mit them to subject their child to Bimran tyranny."

Nobody was gasping or wriggling—everybody but me had expected this—but the breathing around the table had changed slightly. Everything a little tighter. This was strong stuff, even for initiates.

Vailid reared her head proudly. "They escaped with me, a tiny infant. Don't ask how they escaped. Their method was unique, and it is no longer available. But it is no longer needed. All you need to know is that they did escape—with me. I grew up, friends, knowing what freedom is. Not only knowing, but experiencing it." She turned, a smooth, slow, whole-body rotation, to look at us one by one, and centered on me again. "And I came back to Bimran." Pause. "And I came back to Bimran, friends. You see me here. You touch me here." She shot out both her arms, reaching toward the two ends of the table, and people got briefly tangled in each other's robes as they stretched to touch her spread fingers or the backs of her hands. I didn't move. She noticed—I was sure of that—but she didn't give me any pointed look. She took her hands back and people resettled themselves.

"I came back," she said. "But I did not come back alone. I came to bring freedom to my people. I came to bring freedom to all who are willing to accept it." She folded her arms suddenly, hands together at her throat, enclosing her-self in a blue sheath. "On Bimran, we are taught that if we are good we may be selected for Bliss; if we are bad, we may be selected for Punishment. We are taught that it is not for us to decide whether our actions are good or bad; that will be determined by a Selector. We are taught that the Selector acts for God. Apparently God *wants* certain people—chosen we do not know how—to be dragged out of their homes and tortured—tortured for as many years and hours and seconds and nanoseconds as their abused brains are capable of receiving pain stimuli. Apparently God wants certain other people to be led from their homes to facilities very much resembling the torture chambers and there given treatment that is exactly similar—except, we are told, that it produces extreme pleasure instead of extreme pain. On Bimran, people expect this kind of treatment. On Bimran, people are taught to cower, to lie low, and to wait for whatever may be done to them. But out *there*, friends—" she flung her draped arms out and up, rocking her head back and from side to side, aiming all eyes but mine to the far corners of the ceiling "—out there in the galaxy, there is freedom! People don't wait for a Selector; they select their own fate."

Her arms sank to her sides, but she held herself so upright that she could look benignly down on us. "Then why have I come to tell you this? Is it to make you realize how unlucky you are, how oppressed? Is it to urge you to escape from Bimran as my parents did? No; something much better, much easier. I have told you that I did not come back to Bimran alone." A sudden smile split her face. "I brought freedom with me!"

The circle stirred, murmuring little sounds of satisfaction. This was what they'd come for. Vailid went on, gentle now, moving her hands in a slow dance that became an untouching embrace. "Freedom is here, friends, here on Bimran, here in this room. All you need to do is take it. Reach out and take it. Reach in and take it. Friends, none of us need to fear a harsh reality imposed on us from outside—by Selectors, by some vengeful, punishing God, by other people's ideas of what we should do and be. We make our own reality." She stopped dead, waited, waited, waited. Around the table, breathing was hushed. "We make our own reality!" she shouted, and flung her arms wide.

I was keeping a studiously straight face. Maybe it comes of being a starshipper, but I don't like performances that are supposed to convince me of something. If you want to entertain me, perform; if you want to convince me, give me reasons. But I didn't want to antagonize anybody. Best to look as noncommittal as possible.

Which wasn't noncommittal enough. Vailid's gaze stroked me thoughtfully, passing by and then coming back to my face. "Some of you," she said, her voice sinking to a lower key as her arms drifted back to her sides, "already know what that means. We make; our own; reality. Like prisms, we change whatever falls upon us. We can convert the bland whiteness of our lives into a rainbow." She smiled again, but this time the smile came very slowly—first just a stir of her lips, spreading and growing until she was positively radiating, straight at me. "But for those who don't yet understand the plasticity of reality, something else comes first—something easier to grasp." She lowered her gaze and her smile, gesturing with her open hands at the table, or at the white sheet of writing paper in front of her. "Here." And she sank lower into her cushion.

All around the table there was a general shifting and settling, as people responded with their bodies to Vailid's movement. Several hands straightened their papers.

"Does everyone have a handwriter?" Vailid asked. "We have extras here."

Rustles, as people brought out handwriters and patched subvocalizers to their throats. Vailid had her own writer ready, stroking it a few times across her paper as if to practice her moves. "I said that I did not return alone," she told us (told me, in particular). "I said that I came with freedom. But I came also with personal friends. They are with me now." People on both sides of me were breathing eagerly. Vailid's smile changed—knowing, I would call it, and almost affectionate. "No one is ever forced to be alone," she said. "There are entities unfettered by the constraints that we accept, unfettered by human artifacts like the speed of light—or time." I stared at her. Did she know she was talking to a starshipper? "Friends, those entities are all around us. They can speak to us; they can speak through us. I ask you now to share an experience—with me, with them, with each other. Let us make our minds as smooth, as blank, as open as these sheets of paper. Let's relax—let go—let go of your muscles—open yourself, smooth yourself, blank yourself—let them come, let them enter, let them speak—"

I had my own handwriter out, poised on my paper. In this kind of atmosphere, even the Rainbow Man had better blend in. Vailid's voice faded to a murmur and died away. The other listeners sat in what were doubtless blank, smooth, and open postures—their eyes lowered to their papers or lifted to the ceiling or staring straight and glazed, or rolled back to show nothing but whites, their lips barely parted, waiting for the word to come.

It came first to Vailid. She stiffened; and nobody at the table was too rapt to notice. Eyes came up or down to focus on her expectantly.

Her face changed. If she had been performing before, she was real now. The corners of her mouth had drawn down, making her face look longer and older. Her eyes narrowed as she studied us. "So here we are on Bimran," she said sardonically. "And what can we do about it? That's what most of you are thinking, isn't it?" Her voice was so different that it came as a shock, even though I'd been expecting a change. You'd need a pretty good sound analyzer to prove it was produced by the same vocal apparatus.

"Who is speaking?" the woman who had welcomed me in asked hesitantly.

That elicited a little, scornful laugh. "Who is speaking? Good question. The body of a woman named Vailid, about whom I know very little except that she can access me. The 'I' who hears your question and responds through her mouth is Corriogaskula. That's the short version of my name. *Please* don't shorten it any further."

I was already beginning to think I might like Corriogaskula better than Vailid. Somebody else cleared his throat nervously before asking, "Are you a Bimranite?"

"God forbid! I was born—that is, by your system of reckoning, I *will* be born some thirty thousand years from now—almost on the far side of the galaxy from here. But Bimranites are like any other spiritual beings; they are capable of contacting reality."

People were leaning forward intently, some of them taking notes with their handwriters. "Vailid says we make our own reality," someone ventured.

"That's true in a sense. Vailid has some sound ideas and considerable knowledge."

I bent my head, not to show my grin too obviously. This might not be Vailid's voice, but it was certainly coming out of Vailid's mouth, with Vailid's permission. But when I looked up again, Vailid's eyes were fixed on me with what was presumably Corriogaskula's expression of slightly bored disdain.

"We make our own reality," Corriogaskula's voice continued dryly, "in the sense that we modify reality in our perception of it—and in the more important sense that the reality we perceive affects the reality perceived by others. Do you follow me? I don't think so. I'm telling you that even Bimranites, working together, can change the universe."

Nobody objected to this abuse of Bimranites. In fact, they seemed to love the message. "Tell us how," someone pleaded.

"How? By believing what you pretend to believe. Mind can touch mind across time and space—you may not know that, but I certainly do, since I find myself here and now. Mind can direct and control the behavior of matter—as I speak through Vailid, and as even Bimranites are taught to heal their physical wounds. What you believe is true affects what is true. Please note that I did not say 'What you *want* to be true affects' et cetera. I've encountered beings in some times and spaces whose idea of changing the universe is to say 'Oh, my, wouldn't it be nice if—' And others who are apparently convinced that lust guarantees copulation." Vailid-Corriogaskula's face tightened to a terrible smile. "Most of you should be able to ascertain from an examination of your own lives that wanting something does not make it happen."

"What can we do, then?" a voice asked timidly.

"That's for you to answer, isn't it? I don't know your individual capabilities. I know that when a planetful of people believe that they live in a totalitarian universe governed by retribution, their little piece of the universe becomes totalitarian and retributive. If you believe—which is not the same thing as thinking you believe, or wanting to believe— that the universe is benign, that there is no such thing as sin or punishment, and that you are free to create your own lives, then you will find it so. The universe you've been taught to believe in is a purely arbitrary construction. 'Natural law,' so-called, is a human concept, and the natural laws you think you are bound by are as unnecessary and as arbitrary as the governmental laws that Bimran has escaped. Some of you would say that you believe only what your perceptions and your mathematics tell you must be true; but you are wrong. Your perceptions and your mathematics tell you only what you believe can be true—you and the people around you."

Vailid's body stiffened again. Little gasps of protest came from the listeners. "Remember," Corriogaskula's voice said, so tightly it sounded almost strangled, "doubt and belief are simple opposites. Don't doubt what you can do. Believe it."

A violent shudder ran through her—like a shake-dance on Namsatt Nine, I thought—and then she blinked and sighed and lifted her blank sheet of paper, frowning at it. Corriogaskula, obviously, was gone. "I thought I must have written something," Vailid said. "Can some of you tell me what has just been happening here?"

The whole group came alive. Blue-swathed arms flourished and voices interrupted each other eagerly. "You accessed!" "A wonderful entity—" "Corriogastrula—" "—gaskula! From the other side of the galaxy—" "Thirty thousand years—" "I took notes." "So did I. He said you had sound ideas and wonderful knowledge and we should listen to you carefully." "Oh, did you perceive a masculine manifestation? I thought feminine." "That's exactly what he said—you perceive what you believe!"

I felt a real chill, as if somebody had activated a cold-air outlet behind me. What was the matter with these people? Didn't they know a personality flip when they saw one? Surely multiple personality was one of the basic phenomena that any theory of psychology had to deal with. Surely nobody, even on Bimran, believed in possession by spirits— spirits of the dead or the unborn, demons, gods, animals, people in the next room or on the other side of the galaxy, whatever. Surely that was one of the really primitive tricks of religion, like sacrifices to feed the gods. I'd been on worlds where people cultivated multiple personalities as a form of relaxation (though I never saw the point of it myself, since one personality can't feel another's experiences directly). Everybody knew—didn't they?—that for some individuals in some societies it's a real survival strategy to act out fantasies in the most emphatic way, by becoming somebody else.

Gradually the furor calmed. It was time, Vailid announced, for serious meditation. She should not be the only one to receive a message. People settled again to their blank sheets. "If you like," the woman who'd ushered me in said softly, "you can share my sunlight."

"Thank you," I said, with what must have been a very blank look, "but I'm just leaving."

"It's a very fine one. I got it from Vailid herself." She was pulling a loose balloon bag from under the table.

Someone on her other side shushed her, but it was too late. I saw what she was taking out of the bag: one of my golden weaves—sold, I thought I remembered, to the Puffer Club.

"What are you going to do with it?" I asked.

The woman who had brought it out looked uncertainly back and forth between me and her neighbor, not understanding where I fitted into all this. "It's wonderful for meditation," she told me. "We call them sunlights. They come from—oh!" She had gotten an inkling. "They come from offworld," she finished lamely. "But you—you must be the Rainbow Man! You made them!"

"I make them to sell," I said. "I don't know or care what people do with them. And I *am* leaving now. Have fun."

That probably wasn't the right thing to say, but I wasn't interested in any more social niceties. I just wanted out. I'd been talking too loud, too. Everybody had turned to watch. I stood up and headed for the curtained doorway.

"We are grateful to you, *Trojan* Liss," Vailid's voice rang out. "Never forget our gratitude."

I made it into the entry room with a feeling that my spinal fluid was suddenly supercooled. I shed my blue robe onto the pile, retrieved my footboard, and peered out into the night. Suddenly I didn't like the prospect. There were more things on Bimran than met the tourist's eye, and Vailid was probably just one of them. Sarelli hadn't done me any favor. I looked both ways along the dim street, and a resentful shudder ran down my back. Why didn't Bimranites light their streets? Well, of course, this was Bimran; if you wanted light, you were supposed to provide your own.

Vailid had known who I was all along. And that last line had sounded like trouble. *Never forget our gratitude.* The implication was that I might pretty seriously want to forget it.

It was so quiet I could hear the noises my footboard made on the rock-hard Bimran pavement: *clatterscrapethumpscrape,* muted but continuous. What light there was came from the starry sky—not much cloud cover tonight, I was glad to see—and from an occasional doorway with a luminous threshold. There might or might not be conscious minds behind the dark walls on each side; Bimran viewports were usually equipped with lightproof shutters.

I knew roughly where my quarters lay from here—at least I thought I did—but I hadn't paid much attention to the route. Sarelli had been leading the way. Still, if I kept on in this direction I should soon be coming to the river, and then all I had to do was follow it north into the neighborhood I knew.

Never forget our gratitude. That probably translated to *Never forget that we're all in the same capsule.* If I told tales that got

Vailid and her group into trouble I might find myself in the midst of it. After all, I'd participated in their meeting, and they were using my artifacts.

But what trouble could I get them into? There were no laws on Bimran. Can you have subversives when there's no structure to subvert? The street forked into three curving lanes, and I hesitated an instant before I took the middle one. With a little luck, it would bring me more directly to the river.

But of course there *was* a structure, and of course what Vailid preached *was* subversive. Two structures, in fact, working together; institutional synergy. The Migration Control system kept people on Bimran, and the Selection system kept them in line. It doesn't take a cabal of power-hungry tyrants to make a tyranny; a consensus of active moralists is good enough.

The pavement was rougher here, and my footboard noisier. I strained my hearing for the first murmur of the river. If Bimranites didn't make their toxic streets so rough, their toxic footboards wouldn't be so loud. Selection didn't apply to offworlders; Vailid couldn't threaten me with that. But there were probably ways of making life very uncomfortable for improper persons. Where *was* that river?

My footboard stopped. Was I listening so hard I had given it an accidental signal? I trod hard on the accelerator. It was dead.

I knelt to fiddle with the board in the dark. No damage that I could feel, no response to pressure. Well, footboards weren't all that much speedier than legs. I stood up and tucked the board under my arm—really I should get a Bimran-style shoulder carry—glancing back the way I had come. There was a light coming toward me.

Whoever it was had a quieter footboard than mine, and

a faster one. Whoever or whatever; I couldn't tell whether it was a person or a mobile mechanism. Robots weren't used much on Bimran, aside from mechanized receptionists like the voice at Vailid's meeting. The light was a shielded beam that showed nothing about its source but the point of origin, which seemed to be at a plausibly human height or not much more. I started off briskly, trying to look like somebody who knew the neighborhood. I wasn't scared—not actively scared—just uneasy enough to activate an old starshipper reflex, something I'd learned several planets back: never admit weakness to the planetbound. There's no way you can know them well enough to predict when they can be trusted.

There wasn't any scrape and thump, just a soft hiss and the light suddenly laying my clearcut shadow on the pavement ahead. Now was the time to turn, either to give simple Bimran friendliness a try ("Hey, do you know how to fix footboards?") or to strike a self-defense pose. (I didn't know how to fight, but on Ishi Three I'd learned to fake some opening positions.) But either way would be admitting weakness.

My shadow condensed and swerved. The hiss died to a slow scrape. I felt the presence beside me. The light blinded me, and I squinted and grimaced, glad to have honest annoyance to put into my voice. "Can't you turn that down a little?"

No answer, except a *skrit skrit* from the footboard as it moved slowly past me. I could have reached out and touched the rider—if there was a rider. The light turned steadily, staying full on me. Then it went out.

In the total blackness I stopped dead for an instant before I took a quick step sideways—which would have been already too late if there were anything to evade. But the watcher's footboard hissed away from me down the street, and in a minute or two I could make out a vague shape in the dimness, just before it disappeared—around a corner, perhaps, or through a doorway.

I walked on, shaken, and stumbled with my second step. Somebody had wanted a good look at me, and the inspection was over—at least for now. No use hoping I hadn't been recognized; everybody knew the Rainbow Man. Experimentally, I set down my footboard and got on. It worked perfectly.

≈ 10 ≈

There is no place for secrecy in Selection. Ideally the observation process should be unobtrusive, but Selectors must always act on the assumption that an observed individual is aware of the observation or may become so at any moment.

—*From* Revised Manual for Selectors,
Working Draft, Chapter 3.

Yes, I've heard about Vailid," Leona said. "Bunch of bunk, if you ask me. They like to say you make your own reality. Well, in my experience, you can drop out of one reality but you always drop into another one. Still, they don't seem to harm anybody but themselves."

"Are you sure about that?"

She looked at me keenly. "All right, Liss, what haven't you told me yet?"

"When I left there, somebody followed me. Followed me, deactivated my footboard, and took a very good look at me."

She frowned. "Somebody who came out of the same door you did?"

"I don't know. I didn't notice anything till I was maybe two hundred meters down the street."

"Hmp. I don't know what to tell you, Liss—except I think you'd be smart to stay away from those people. If they ever attract a Selector's attention, they'll be in trouble. Nobody knows exactly what they believe—I doubt if *they* do—but it sure as slud isn't orthodox." She twisted her head sideways, dissatisfied, and rubbed the back of her neck. "Funny, though. I never heard of them doing anything sinister like following people in the dark. Didn't think they were organized enough."

"Where did they get all that blue fabric, Leona? Nobody wears blue on Bimran. Where did they get a robot receptionist? I mean, it's not just a few crackpots. It must be a fairly prosperous movement."

"Oh, I expect everybody chips in," Leona said. "They've been supporting Vailid for at least a couple of Bimran years." She chuckled. "Now, for Rab's sake, girl, don't start looking gloomy. I've renewed my visitor's permit five times already, and I mean to keep on renewing it. Bimran is the best place *I've* ever seen to be a resident alien."

I laughed. "I'm not about to run away from it. I like it here, too."

"Good," she said warmly. "I wouldn't want to see you leave."

The look in her eyes was a starshipper's look, measuring me prospectively for memory. Which is a euphemistic way of saying for death. A surge of anger came up in me like acid—equal parts of anger for the constraints of space-time and the people who thought they could escape those constraints by ignoring them. "They think they've got instantaneous communication, Leona—astral projection, distance-independent telepathy, I don't know what. Vailid did a personality flip and they called it accessing an entity on the other side of the galaxy."

Leona shrugged expansively. "Souls. Souls is what they think they've got. Vailid attracts the kind of people who think the real you is some immaterial sort of thing like a baby god, that got mixed up temporarily with your body and can do just as well without it. Bunch of toxic bunk."

"Yes," I said. "I think it is." A chill wriggled my spine. Way back on Namsatt Nine I'd seen what happens to human identities when you take pieces of their physiology out.

"If you ask me," Leona said, "there are two kinds of those soul-junkies: the ones who say, 'I didn't get a fair deal this time around, I want to collect damages,' and the ones who say, 'I didn't get a fair deal this time around, I want another try.' Those who opt for heaven and those who opt for reincarnation." She snorted something like a laugh. "Funny part of it is, they all think they're entitled to a fair deal."

I jumped up and crossed her little room to give her a hug, bending over her mushroom. It's wonderful how a dose of common sense can reconcile you to the universe.

"Mind you," Leona said, when I stopped smothering her—a puffsuit does get in the way sometimes— "most Bimranites are smarter than that. I don't know what your Vailidites would say if she died and somebody grew about a thousand clones out of her cells. Would that be a thousand souls, or one? Or none, considering the clones were stewed up from a vacated corpse? Identical souls, or different? Or maybe one clone with a soul and nine hundred ninety-nine sisters walking around soulless? Thank Athena, most Bimranites don't swallow that soul-juice."

I clapped my hands together. "That's it! I never figured it out before, Leona. That's why they have to have Selectors."

She sniffed, unimpressed. "What, you mean why they don't leave the Bliss and Punishment up to God? That's pretty obvious. They're smart enough to see their God's not taking care of it in *this* life, and too smart to doublethink themselves into believing it'll get taken care of in another. Selection makes a lot of sense from their point of view."

"Yes." I shuddered again. "I wish it didn't."

Longer life, faster travel: those were the two things people yearned for badly enough to invent theologies. Quantitative, both of them. And maybe *that* was the difference between starshippers and planetbound. On a starship, you learn to accept space-time as is, no refunds or replacements. But the planetbound don't have to deal with time and space raw; they can make up stories about them.

Still, we're all caught in the same web, planets and starships alike. Perceptual universe as museum: Sarelli had a good point. Every one of us is separated by instants or light-millennia from anybody else's actuality. That's why every attempt at interstellar empire or federation disintegrates as fast as it grows. The only really successful large-scale enterprises are one-way systems like the Linguistic Academy and the Galactic Standards Institute, that simply broadcast their data and don't depend on feedback. And starships; starships weaving their continuity through the galaxy, making it worthwhile for other people to comply with standards and usage lists. Starshippers are probably the closest thing to souls this universe has to offer. I could see why Vailid's friends preferred a Corriogaskula.

I didn't see Sarelli for a few days. That wasn't unusual, but this time I found myself wondering if he was avoiding me. Communication on Bimran, as far as I could tell, was very haphazard. There were message services, used mostly for business, that would send visual or aural messages for a small fee "anywhere on Bimran"—meaning, it turned out, to any other message office, which would then undertake to hand-deliver them. To me this sounded one step more primitive than jungle drums; but Bimranites didn't like communications (or anything else) intruding into their private spaces.

They didn't use either live or recorded projections; when you saw a person, you knew it was the real thing.

Whatever that gliding shape in the night had done to my footboard seemed to have aftereffects. The board had picked up a bad habit of losing power without warning, usually on a turn. I took it to a footboard shop—not the one where I'd bought it. The shopowner ran it through her tester and shook her head. "Sorry," she said. "I'll credit you for the value of the materials and make you a new one, if you want to get rid of this now. Or you can ride it another week or two, if you don't mind getting dumped a few times. They don't last forever, you know."

"But I bought this new," I protested. "They told me it was good for at least two years of normal use."

She raised a skeptical eyebrow. "If that's so, I'd complain to whoever you bought it from. It does *look* like a new board; but the power's almost gone."

"And you can't repair it?"

"There's no way to repair the power. When it's gone, it's gone." She hefted the board in her hands. "Do you want the credit?"

"Thanks, I'll keep the board."

But I didn't take it right away to the shop where I'd bought it. Partly, it was the uncomfortable feeling you get when the locals may or may not be cheating you, and you don't want to make a fool of yourself. Mostly, it was the conviction that if my footboard had really been zapped by the silent watcher in the night, I'd be better off if I didn't talk about it in public.

There was a little fruit shop north of the Park where they sold rough-skinned, unappetizing-looking fruits so juicy you could stick a drinking tube into one and suck out the sweet slushy pulp. I had just settled at an unoccupied table—I wasn't feeling very sociable—and plugged my drinking tube into the convenient dimple at one end of a fruit, when two people approached me, fruits in hand.

"Nice day," one of them said. "May we join you?" They both immediately sat down.

I knew that voice. This was the woman who had sat next to me at Vailid's table, the one who had offered me a sunlight. "Apparently so," I said.

She smiled brightly. "We were just finishing our fruits when we saw you come in. And I said, 'Oh, we must go over and apologize.' " Her cheek dimpled as she sucked her drinking tube.

"That's not necessary." I'd almost said, *Apologize for what?*, but that would be inviting her to talk about the meeting at Vailid's.

She sucked, smiled, sucked, and smiled again. "Well, of course, everyone knows you by sight. I'm so sorry I didn't recognize you the other evening. I can't think why not."

That was carrying politeness to a ridiculous degree. "It's the clothes," I said.

"Oh, yes, of course." She squeezed her fruit experimentally. "Oh, how rude of me!—My name is Shray, and this is my friend Morit. I don't think you've been introduced."

I recognized him—yes, the blue robes did make a difference—a thin-faced man from the other side of Vailid's table. "My name is Liss," I said firmly, in case they only knew me as the Rainbow Man.

He smiled instantly. (He had been watching me till then with what seemed anxious eyes.) "We thought perhaps we could get together for a chat, Liss. Since we have interests in common."

"Do we?"

His smile closed up like an emergency seal. "Well, we assumed—" And opened again. "Other worlds are always fascinating. Other worlds, other lives. I'm tremendously interested in your opinions."

Shray sucked at her empty fruit, and laughed, startled at the noise it made. "Oh, excuse me." Her eyes darted here and there. "I was thinking we might pack a lunch and hike out to the hills past the spaceport. That is, if you like walking—"

"And if you don't," Morit put in, "we could take a float-car. Our treat, of course; you'd be our guest."

"I'm afraid I'll be occupied for the foreseeable future," I said. "Thanks anyway."

Morit shot a glance at Shray. "Actually, you'd be doing us a favor," he told me. "We're not married, you see—just friends. We've been wanting to picnic up there, but we can't very well go alone."

"Why not?" I asked.

Shray laughed nervously. "It wouldn't look right, would it? I mean, it's such a lonely place up there. There might be nobody else at all."

Something focused. "I know you. I mean I saw you before. Before that night at Vailid's. You were watching tourists shoot the river, and an Ishian gave you money. You were carrying a blue flower. That was a recognition signal, wasn't it?"

Shray was blinking like a pulse light. "Why, I—Yes, it was a signal—I had no idea *you* were there—"

In case I'd had any doubt, she was showing me what amateurs Vailid's conspirators were. I'd walked right into her transaction, and she didn't recognize me. Morit was squeezing his fruit determinedly.

"What do you do with my gold weaves?" I asked. "Your so-called sunlights?"

Morit's eyes blinked shut, as if a sudden flash of light had caught them. Shray glanced around at the other tables. "Well," she said with decided cheerfulness, "we could talk about things like that, up in the hills. All sorts of things. Do say we can get together some day soon."

"I'd be more likely to," I said, "if I hadn't been followed."

That shook them. Morit's eyes popped open and closed slowly again. Shray's mouth shaped the word, but she didn't quite speak it. *Followed,* I gathered, was not something you said in public. Instead, she stood up, saying brightly, "Well, I'll leave you men to talk about things," and walked away from us.

Morit dared (or was it condescended?) to look at me. "Well," he said, sharing Shray's brightness, "would you care to stroll? Only if you're ready to go, of course."

"No, thanks," I said. "I'd rather sit here." That was reacting like a Bimranite. It wouldn't look right, would it, to go strolling with a possible subversive. Here in the fruit shop there were plenty of witnesses to the fact that Shray and Morit had approached me, not vice versa. I gazed defiantly around the room, and met the eyes of one of those witnesses—alone at a table, drab black and quiet, Doron.

≈ 11 ≈

Every individual is presumed virtuous until proved otherwise. Selectors should understand, however, that this is a temporary expedient, pending the development of more precise Selection techniques. Compassion begs us to err on the side of Bliss rather than on that of Punishment; reason informs us that it is not permissible to err at all.
—From Revised Manual for Selectors,
Working Draft, Conclusions.

First reactions are funny. The only coherent thought I had was *Don't,* and that was aimed at Doron. Above all else, I didn't want him to follow Shray out of the shop, like some scandalmonger's paid spy trailing a politician. Beyond that, I didn't feel anything. I was floating in free-fall, waiting for gravity to kick in from one direction or another. I was ready to be very, very angry—that was if Doron did follow Shray—or glad and amused, or sad as spaceport good-byes, or simply disappointed and separate. "A Selector is watching you," I said to Morit.

He shut his eyes and opened them again. I had the feeling I kept giving Morit stimuli he didn't have responses for. He stood up, nodded to me, and left without a word and without looking around.

I waited, cradling my fruit in both hands. I watched Doron watch Morit leave and then look back to me. He stood up and came to me without a smile. Gravity kicked in and I felt myself glow at him. "Nice day," he said.

"Sit down, Doron."

"I wish I could. I'm sorry, Liss, I'm working."

"So I noticed." My glow was shifting toward the anger end of the spectrum. I stood up. "I don't like this place. Let's get outside."

Outside, I expected him to scan the street and the adjacent Park; but if he did, it was so unobtrusively I didn't notice. "I'm going this way," he said, pointing north. There were plenty of people about, going north, south, and every direction between, and maybe one of them was Morit and another one Shray. I didn't want to know.

"I'll walk with you," I said.

A quick beam of a smile. "Good," he said warmly. "I thought—I was afraid you were angry." We began to walk.

"I am angry."

"I'm sorry." Not an apology, just a statement of fact.

"I'm not being particularly fair," I said. "I just haven't sorted out my reactions. But I do know I don't like seeing you interfere in other people's lives. *I'm* sorry, Doron."

He was silent for a long moment. "One of the first things," he said then, "that Selectors have to learn is that we can't interfere in people's lives. We can't tell anyone what to do or not to do. Even harder, we can't make decisions for anyone except ourselves."

"Not *for* anyone, just *about* them," I said.

"The people we Select have already made their own decisions," he said. "We present them with the consequences."

"Selector?" a new voice said beside us, so near that I jerked. How had anybody gotten that close without my noticing? The speaker was massive as well as tall, and flamboyant in spite of the sober black garb. Red beards, from what I'd seen, were as unusual on Bimran as bright clothes.

Doron had lifted his eyes to the newcomer. "Yes?" It was neutral, it was equable, it was the tone of patient interest that seemed so quintessentially Doron, and I realized how much more intimate our conversations had become without my exactly noticing. Doron was reserved with me, maybe, but not one tenth as reserved as he had been at the beginning, or as he was now with other people. I couldn't tell from those two words exchanged whether Redbeard was a complete stranger or an old acquaintance.

"May I have a word with you?"

"Of course," Doron said, and turned to me. "Perhaps I'll see you again in the Park."

I'd never been dismissed so abruptly before in my life. "Oh. Yes," I said. "Perhaps so." Redbeard's eyes—sharp, tawny eyes in a net of squint lines—focused me and turned away.

The only intelligible information I was left with, as I watched them walk north away from me, was that whatever Redbeard might be to Doron he was certainly no stranger.

Sarelli and I couldn't miss each other for long. The Rainbow Man and the black flash, we were both too obvious. So I wasn't surprised when we spotted each other on the street the next day, a hundred meters apart, both on foot and headed straight for contact. We were both smiling when we got there. "Hey," I said. "Why didn't you warn me about Vailid?"

"Should I have warned you?"

"You bet you should have!"

He looked interested. "Why is that?"

I didn't say whatever I'd meant to say. "Aren't we over-due for a lesson?" I said instead, and he turned instantly and we walked together toward the Park. *If they ever attract a Selector's attention they'll be in trouble,* Leona had said. And it looked very much like they'd attracted a Selector's attention. Shray and Morit weren't my favorite people; but why should I tell a Bimranite—even Sarelli—that other Bimranites sounded subversive? "I trusted you," I said. "I didn't think you'd take me to anything boring."

He tilted his face skyward for a laugh. "Good," he said.

"You want me to be bored?"

He turned toward me, half dancing as he walked. "Are you bored, Liss?"

"Not now."

"Good!"

I laughed, honestly happy for the first time since he'd left me on Vailid's doorstep. "You mean you wanted me to find out there's something more boring than normal Bimran life?"

"Is that a question?"

"Is that an answer?"

We chortled together. "Mind you," Sarelli said, "I don't know what Vailid preaches. But I've known some of the people she preaches to, and I have the impression they believe the theological equivalent of mushfruit."

"Maybe that's why I couldn't tell *what* they believe." *Never forget our gratitude.* My happiness felt a little thinner.

Sarelli stopped and started on again, a pulsar-flash of stillness in his sleek black motion. "Tell me, Liss. Do you ever wonder why the Commandments are all negative?"

"What makes you think I know your Commandments?"

He flung back his head, mouth open in silent laughter. "Oh, what indeed? The axiom of our philosophy, Rainbow Man. All human beings know the Commandments—in their hearts."

I made what I intended to be a rude noise, though you never know if it works with locals. "If I have any commandments stowed away in my heart, I don't think they're negative."

He turned his grin to me for a moment, his brows like sketched curves on a very tentative graph. "Then can they be commandments?"

"Probably not. I can do without commandments."

"Can you, Rainbow Man?"

"Don't call me that."

This time he let out a trickle of laughter. "You see? A negative commandment."

I exploded into laughter of my own. "I give up. Why are commandments always negative?"

Both his hands danced, fingers snapping victory. "Simple. Because voluntary action can't be coerced. Coerced action is not voluntary."

"And salt is salty. That's a truism."

"Is there any truth that's not a truism?" He flashed me one of his instant stares, speculation in a nutshell.

"Stand still a minute," I said. "I'm tired of walking."

He jigged around me. "Then why didn't you bring your footboard?"

"Blast footboards!" I laughed, embarrassed to hear myself so vehement. "No, I think what I really want is for you to stop moving. Can Sarelli have mass without velocity?"

"Do you mind if I vibrate a little?" But he had already stopped still, uncannily still.

"All right," I said, "tell me these toxic four Commandments. What do they command?"

"Abstention," he said. "Four things are forbidden to humans; only four."

Four, out of the incalculable range of human actions. I became as still as Sarelli. "What are they?"

"Idolatry, murder, abuse, and fornication."

I hooted with laughter. "I thought they were supposed to be so simple anybody could understand them."

The brow curves steepened. "Starshippers excepted, Liss? You don't understand?"

"Two out of four words I never heard before. What's 'idolatry'? What's 'fornication'?"

"Idolatry is the worship of pseudo-gods. Fornication is what I decline to do with you, Rainbow Man."

I stood there looking at him, sharp-edged Sarelli, and his eyes got more and more transparent as I looked. Sarelli, Sarelli, you could have told me. He patched a sneer to his mouth for balance. "And that's why you decline?" I asked him. "Because of the Commandments?"

"Yes," he said. "That's an answer. There could be other answers, but that's the one I'm giving you."

I came out of a plant shop, still adjusting a potful of yellow blooms in my new shoulder carry, and almost walked into Morit. It was three days since I'd seen him blink his way out of the fruit shop, and I'd been thinking about him. We did a little dance of politeness, getting ourselves sorted out, and then he fell into step beside me. "Nice day," he said.

"Do you believe that crap?" I asked him. "I don't mean 'Nice day,' I mean Vailid's line—spiritual time-travel, anything you believe is real, all that stuff. Do you believe it?"

He looked at me and looked away. "Vailid is wonderful," he said. "Very impressive."

"Does that mean you believe it? Colliogarrula and all that?"

"I think it's very convincing. You've seen one example, but we've seen many. Corriogaskula is not the first entity she's accessed for us. Several of us have received written communications."

"Written? Oh, right." The blank paper, the handwriters.

"We can't deny the evidence of our own senses," Morit added.

"I thought that was exactly what you did do. Natural laws are an illusion and so on. If you believe time runs backward, you get younger."

"That's true. But you see, it works both ways. The reality we perceive is real because of our collective belief. When our beliefs change, so does reality, and therefore so do our perceptions."

I broke stride for a moment—the result of a quickly squelched impulse to stop in my tracks and argue with him. He wouldn't want to hear how many worlds with different belief systems I'd seen the same laws operating in. There's no use shouting at a deaf ear. "Does that mean you want to change Bimran?" I asked.

He didn't answer for a moment. But it wasn't one of Doron's thoughtful silences, figuring out the theologico-moral implications before he answered; it was just waiting till we got past an old woman (old man?) going the opposite direction. "Nice day," we all said like automatic greeting systems.

Morit cleared his throat. "I believe we *are* changing Bimran."

"So you don't like the way Bimran is now? You don't like Selection?" I was getting heated about it, though I kept my voice cool. I hadn't seen Doron since that day in the fruit shop, either.

"I do not and cannot believe that God wants us to be tortured," Morit said softly.

"Who do you mean by 'us'?"

"Why, I mean all of us, all humans. We're God's own children."

"But people *are* tortured."

He pursed his lips. When Bimranites pursed their lips, it generally meant *What does it matter?* On the *Trojan*, it meant *How about a kiss?* "So it appears," he said. "I wonder if those who actually suffer don't invite it."

"I understand that's the principle," I said. "Don't Selectors say the people Selected get what they were asking for?"

He closed his eyes for an instant. "I mean it quite literally," he said. "They suffer exactly what they want to suffer." I noticed it wasn't *I wonder if* anymore.

"Let me get this straight," I said "Selectors think that everybody selected for Punishment deserves it and knew what they were letting themselves in for. But you say Punishment isn't even punishment—they enjoy it?"

"It *is* punishment. They're punishing themselves. It's what they want, and that's why God allows it. Those of them who actually suffer."

"What do you mean 'who actually suffer'? You think some of them are just pretending?"

"I mean that what looks like suffering to outsiders may be something quite different."

"And how do you know why God does anything?" I'd been on Bimran so long, I didn't even bother qualifying every question with *if God exists.*

"What would be the point," he said, "of imagining an omnipotent God who is not also loving and compassionate?"

"Isn't that sort of like 'What's the point of imagining magnetic fields?' . . . I thought thinking was supposed to be figuring out how things really are, not just dreaming up how you'd like them to be."

He pursed his lips again. "I simply mean that God must be good, and therefore no one suffers unwillingly. God wouldn't allow it."

"You mean you *believe* God wouldn't allow it."

"Yes, that's right," he said.

"And *therefore* God wouldn't allow it."

"Well, I—"

We had reached the street I lived on. I paused at the corner. "Right. Good-bye, Morit. Happy believing. Watch out for Selectors."

≈ 12 ≈

*Abuse is the broadest category of action forbidden by the Command-
ments. It includes every form of harm, short of murder, that one
individual can inflict on another. It is not yet clear whether any
human can be completely innocent of this sin.*
> —*From* Revised Manual for Selectors,
> *Working Draft, Chapter 12.*

I didn't want to torment Sarelli. Penis control or no, he had
definitely lied when he'd said I didn't arouse him sexually.
And I was more than willing to admit it worked both
ways. But if his silly Commandments were so important to
him, I wasn't going to play tempter. If there's one commandment a starshipper learns, it's *Don't mess with local mores.*

Sarelli might be afraid of bare skin—mine, at least—but
he wasn't too busy to see a lot of me clothed. He functioned
in two modes. Sometimes he was the sober, patient teacher:
"It's like traveling a hilly road, Liss. Is that something a
starshipper can imagine? There are humps you think you'll
never get over, and then on the other side it's easy. When
you're hurt, the first hump is accepting the hurt—not trying
to pretend it hasn't happened." When he wasn't teaching, he
was a shrewd, prickly playmate, throwing his flashing riddles
like boomerangs. And at the edges of both modes he pushed
teasingly close to another category, something that might be

called friend. Leona had been my friend from the hour I'd met her. And what about Doron? Did he think of me as a friend? Was "friend" a category Selectors had a use for?

"Catch it, Liss!" That was Sarelli's shouted greeting from across the street, followed by a flashing small object hurled overhand. My hands popped up automatically (all those games on the *Trojan*'s exercise deck hadn't been wasted time) and caught it with only a slight fumble. A fist-sized black ball, dense and elastic, with bright points of light spaced around its equator.

"Catch!" he shouted again. I dropped the first ball to catch the second, and threw it back as he loped across the street. He had to reach to catch it, giving me time to pick up the other ball and step backward into the open space of the Park.

"This is revelation!" Sarelli called. He dodged around a speeding footboarder and threw the one ball just as I threw the other. "It comes at you—" (catch and throw) "unexpect-edly—" (catch and throw) "and you deal with it—" (catch and throw) "however you can—" (catch and throw) "and arrange your life around it."

By that time we'd arranged ourselves in a slowly circling, slowly drifting orbit across the Park's springy moss. The dots of light on the balls traced twisting patterns through the air. I laughed. "All right, point taken!" Catch and throw. "Sarelli, you really think that stuff in the museum is revelation?"

"Rainbow Man, you really think light-speed is a limit?"

"It works that way."

"Listen to yourself and hear my answer."

I threw my next ball harder, stressing the rhythm but not breaking it. "Oh, slud, Sarelli!"

"Appropriate comment. What's the matter?"

"How can a skeptic like you believe in God?"

"What makes you think I'm a skeptic?"

"No, answer my question!" I aimed a ball at his head, and he caught it left-handed.

"Isn't it obvious?"

"No, it isn't."

He caught the other ball and kept them both. "Surely it's been obvious at least since qualate physics superseded quantum."

"What does that have to do with it? Come on, throw!"

He feinted with one ball, but didn't let it go. "Human minds can handle quantum, with a little effort. But imagine the shock to mathematicians when mathematics took off without them." He sneered joyously, that Sarelli look of *Isn't stupidity entertaining?* "Although the probability is that they didn't notice." He feinted again, this time with the other hand, and I stamped my foot in mock impatience. "In the old days, machines only manipulated data—it was humans who understood it. Now the closest we can come to understanding our universe is to say, 'Ah, whatever those machines are doing, it works.' Doesn't that speak strongly for the existence of a Creator God?" He feinted and threw, and I fumbled the catch but didn't quite drop it.

"I don't hear it speaking, Sarelli. How do you figure? Here, catch!"

He caught, and brushed the two balls together as if he were getting rid of a fleck of something sticky. "Very straightforwardly, Rainbow Man. Anything so complex and so successful as this universe must have been designed by a superior intelligence—superior to anything inside the design."

"What makes you think it's designed?"

"Inductive reasoning." He hurled a ball, and I caught it

in self-defense. "If every part examined appears to have been designed for a function—or generally several functions—the reasonable conclusion is that the whole thing was designed. It's a classic argument, pretty Liss. Very basic."

It took me several seconds, and two throws, to figure out what he was talking about. "But it's not an argument at all! What you're saying is, 'The world is more complex than anything *I* could design; since I *assume* the world was designed, it must have been done by somebody much smarter than I am.' Why aren't you saying, 'The world is more complex than any design job I know of; looks like it wasn't designed!'? What's the point of calling your assumption a conclusion?" And suddenly I had to duck.

But I'd asked a stupid question, as Leona pointed out to me when I told her about it. "Idiot," she said cheerfully. "The point of calling any assumption a conclusion is to give it the logical authority it doesn't have. But that's not something anybody admits. What did Sarelli say?"

I was pacing around the circumference of the spongy mat she'd found somewhere to soften her hard Bimran floor. "He said if that wasn't a rational conclusion, then neither is ninety-five percent of human reasoning."

Leona laughed from the belly up, sinking farther back into her mushroom. "Right on the dot! Doesn't speak well for human rationality, does it?"

I frowned, puzzling it through as I paced. "All right, tell me this, Leona: Why do people feel better when they feel helpless? I mean, I don't care if they want to assume that the universe was designed by some deity, and then pretend they figured it out by inductive logic; but why do they want to assume it in the first place? Why do they want this super-overseer looking over their shoulder, knowing and potentially controlling everything they think and do?"

"You've got it backwards, Liss. People feel helpless first, then they start looking for the all-purpose parent. That's what their singular-number God is." She made a wry face and drummed her fingertips on her knee. "Don't blame them, girl. If you've never felt helpless, you're even younger than I thought you were." She slapped both knees and began heaving herself up out of the mushroom. "You're as restless as a pulsar, and so am I. You know what the trouble is?"

"Tell me quick!" I knew my trouble; his name was Doron.

"Starshippers are like starships, that's the trouble. They can't stay away from spaceports forever. It's about time for me to mosey across the bridge and see if anything's come in."

"I'll come with you," I said. "How long does it take to walk it?"

Leona chortled. "You don't much care, girl—you just want to go. If you cared how long, you'd have asked first."

"Well, I'm asking now. Humor me."

"Oh, quarter of an hour for a brisk walker. Half an hour serious moseying."

"Let's mosey." Even with Sarelli's help, killing time had become a real problem for me. I wasn't used to that.

We moseyed, chatting idly, looking into shops, exchanging greetings with other strollers, enjoying the faint warmth of the early Bimran autumn. Just before the south bridge we passed a clothes shop. "Come in with me," Leona said. "I need to buy a guardcape. Old one's about as much use in a thunderstorm as an hourglass in free-fall."

"Do they sell bubblesuits?"

"Probably not, but you can ask."

There were no bubblesuits, but while Leona haggled for her guardcape I looked through a pile of uniformly plain walkingsuits, solid brown or solid gray or solid black. Well, why not? Bimranite clothing was drab, but it was functional. And hadn't I bought a damask wraparound on Gantry Four and a totally transparent warmsuit on Old Kossolo? I shook out a brown walkingsuit and held it up against my body. Big enough to cover everything, which was the Bimran idea of a good fit.

"Would you like to try that on?" the shopkeeper asked.

I wrinkled my nose. "No, it's fine. I'll take it." If I actually put it on, or if I thought about it long enough to haggle, chances were I wouldn't buy it. "How much do you want for it in gold?"

Leona threw back her head in a happy cackle. "Good for you, Liss! You can wear it every time you want to be inconspicuous."

On some worlds, spaceports are purely business; the only reason to go there is to get on a ship or to make a profit. On Bimran, visiting the spaceport was one of the things people did for fun, one of the little excursions that Bimranites were always taking. When a starship docked, people gathered from all over the planet to enjoy the occasion, just as they gathered to enjoy a major concert or a really good sweetseed harvest.

Most starships (local regulations permitting) keep a landing module on the ground as long as they're in docking orbit. Deals are struck there, potential problems with the locals are scouted and defused, and it's a handy piece of home for sightseeing crew members to check back with anytime they get nervous. Meanwhile another lander can be ferrying cargo, crew, and visitors up and down as required. Bimranites liked to watch all this from a slight distance, standing a few meters back and keeping politely out of the way while they chattered and pointed and smiled. Between starships, they could watch the little vessels that were the spaceport's main business: shuttles from the Ishian planets and a few other Gemmeus Cluster worlds, carrying tourists and traders. Between shuttles, they came just to see the spaceport. Bimranites were easily pleased.

I hadn't been back here since the day I left the *Trojan,* which was about ten Bimran weeks ago, or something more than two months Galactic Standard. Then it had been a busy place, with a regular stream of floatcars collecting and depositing sightseers and small traders and Ishian and Gantryite tourists from a shuttle that had just docked. Today it was almost empty—a few people repairing a warehouse roof, a few parents showing their children where the shuttles landed, a few idlers like Leona and me—and it was definitely the ugliest thing I'd seen on Bimran. But it caught me hard. That blank stretch of discolored pavement, webbed with cracks, was the pad where the *Trojan's* lander had stood. I tried to visualize the liftoff I hadn't looked back to see. Too late now, Liss.

Leona nodded toward the line of buildings strung out along one side of the landing pad—warehouses, communications, the little office where the Migration Control officer had given me my yellow card. "I ought to drop in there and renew my visitor's permit," she observed. "Then I won't have to bother at the last minute. Doesn't expire for another month, but they'll generally renew it early for you if they think you're serious about staying."

"I'm serious," I said, surprising myself by the way my throat clenched up on the words.

Leona eyed me skeptically. "They don't know that. Wait a few months before you try to convince them."

She was right, of course. And on Bimran there wouldn't be anything as official as a definite timespan during which renewals were accepted. Just having a definite expiration date was probably stressing the system to the limit. "Go ahead," I said. "I want to watch this game."

A dozen or so people in boots, from children to gray-beards, had spread out across the landing pad, calling merrily to each other and brandishing what looked like giant paintbrushes. Leona snorted appreciatively. "That's not a game, that's a work party. I've seen them before." She turned toward the ramp that led to the Migration Control office. "I'll be out in a few minutes. If it takes longer than that, I'm not going to sit still for it. I can always do it another time."

"Go ahead," I repeated absently. I had just noticed that two of the work crew were Shray and Morit.

Three more children emerged from an equipment shelter, pushing a transparent float-tank taller than they were. It bobbed along in front of them to the pad, gently sloshing its load of gray fluid. Morit reached up to activate something near the top, and fluid began to spray out from its underside. With whoops of glee, the children shoved the tank forward and into a wildly spiraling path across the pad, spreading a broad trail of wet gray. The brush-wielders sprang into action, sweeping fluid into cracks. And I walked along the edge of the pad toward a slender figure in dull black.

He had seen me—of course—before I saw him; he was already coming my way under the shady overhang of a warehouse roof. We stopped, face to face, within touching distance. He had the look of somebody who expects to be wounded and is only trying for survival. "Nice day, Liss." It was a wistful hope.

"Are you working?" I asked.

"Yes."

"I didn't know a Selector's work was following people around spying on everything they do."

He smiled wanly. "No. We observe people's activities. That's a small part of what we do. I'd hoped—I'd hoped you understood that by now. From reading the *Manual*."

His eyes were so innocent they looked luminous—dark pools lit from beneath the surface. "I'm sorry," I said, stricken. "I haven't read any of it yet."

"I see," he said. Like a child accepting betrayal. It wasn't just a book he'd put into my hands, that windy day on the bridge; it was his life.

"Not yet," I said. "But I will. I will very soon."

"As you like," he said. "It's your choice, of course." Again the wan smile. "People always have choices, and they always make them. Even when they don't notice it." He turned back into the shadows.

Leona came clumping down the ramp from the Migration Control office, displeased. "For once I'm farsighted enough to renew early, and they won't do it. 'Come back closer to expiration date,' they say. Even on Bimran, a bureaucrat is a bureaucrat."

At the spaceport entrance I turned for one futile look back. Someone else was coming down the Migration Control office ramp—a tall figure with a glint of color above the black. "Leona," I said, "did you see a big man with a red beard in there?"

"Huh?" She broke off her grumbling. "No, just some runty bureaucrats." The figure disappeared under the warehouse eaves.

≈ 13 ≈

Good intentions may produce evil consequences. On the human level, the end is hypothetical; only the means are real.
                              —*From* Revised Manual for Selectors,
                                      Working Draft, Introduction.

It wasn't Doron's voice, but it was Doron's style of voice: cool and serious, determined to get things straight. So the Introduction hit me with a very quiet bang: "We know for a fact that it is right for some people to suffer. The only question is, which ones. We know the fact because we know that God allows suffering and that God is just. It is not necessary to suppose—and we do not—that God explicitly intends every event of space-time. Clearly, however, God maintains a universe in which suffering is common. Suffering is, therefore, an acceptable tool."

My throat felt tight. I deactivated the book. This was what Doron lived by? And yet he wanted me to hear it. I activated.

"On the other hand, the very existence of Commandments proves that not all actions are equally authorized by God. We can obey or disobey God, and thus deserve special reward or special punishment.

"In what might be called the state of nature—that is, in any world without a system of Selection—the distribution of rewards and punishments is in large part morally random. We cannot say that the wicked are regularly punished nor the good regularly rewarded." That was a bit of an understatement, in my opinion, though of course it depended on what you meant by *good* and *wicked.* "Clearly these rewards and punishments are not distributed by God. They result from forces and processes that God does not directly manipulate: the free play of the universe.

"But just as clearly, the existence of natural rewards and punishments—of pleasure and pain—gives us the opportunity to work for God within this free play. We can apply God's standards—the Commandments—to determine who most deserves reward or punishment. This, of course, is the process of Selection."

I deactivated. I didn't have to check the visual to know a capital "S" when I heard one. My quarters seemed smaller than I'd ever noticed—but then, I'd never paced the floor so vigorously. I tossed the *Manual* onto a mushroom. Had it told me anything I hadn't already heard from Doron? Probably not, but now I was hearing it without decoration—without Doron's shining eyes, Doron's furry little beard, Doron's smiles and sadnesses. This was what all the careful Bimran theology came down to: God didn't administer the proper rewards and punishments, so Bimran would. Selectors might not do the administering themselves, but they picked who got what.

I snatched the *Manual* off the mushroom, but I didn't stop pacing. That was just the introduction. What was the real part like? I kept scanning through the visual text, activating the aural whenever I spotted something interesting, or sometimes at random. It wasn't always the same voice. Older, younger, female, androgynous. A real draft, patched together out of separate sections. Committee work—but all too coherent.

A lot of it *was* dry and technical. "Interviewing techniques may be grouped into six major categories. . . . The following expenses will be reimbursed in their entirety. . . . The number of hours spent in altruistic activities must be weighted according to type, manner, and circumstances. . . ." But there were sentences that flashed out at me. "Selectors, though they are not eligible for Selection, must be held to a higher standard than other individuals. . . . Exactly because of the powerful feelings involved, sexual morality is a valid indicator of general morality. . . . A Selector's judgment must never be influenced by personal sympathy or distaste. . . . For God, in a real sense, the end justifies the means."

Entirely private. It would have to be a starshipper he trusted this much; it could never be a Bimranite. I had no vested interest. But by the same token I was an outsider, an unknown. It was a leap of faith on Doron's part to put this book into my hands. *Selectors must be held to a higher standard.* I wasn't going to betray his trust.

But I could still complain to Leona Porlock. The second time in two days I'd been at her door with no excuse except wanting to talk, and she still welcomed me in. That was friendship. "Whatever made humans invent religion in the first place, Leona? I know you have fun with it, but you're not going to tell me it's natural, are you? Most of us get along just fine without any."

"Making connections," Leona said. "That's natural— something humans evolved to do. Doesn't matter how you explain the connections—you'll survive as long as you notice them. Or at least you'll have a better chance."

"Connections? You mean like heat is connected with evaporation?"

She grunted affirmatively. "It's like seeing colors—useful, but there's nothing necessarily rational about it. Most of the time it doesn't make much practical difference whether it's molecules' kinetic energy overcoming surface tension or a thirsty demon slurping up a drink."

"And that makes religion?"

"Well, it makes explanations. After a few hundred thousand years the explainers started separating the molecules from the demons. That gives us science on one side and religion on the other—not necessarily incompatible, just on separate tracks."

"And the religion track evolved from slurping demons to Hermes and Rab and Athena and on to God with a capital G—is that the idea?"

She eyed me sourly. "Got that from Doron, did you? Well, I hate to contradict your Doron, but he's dead wrong. Monotheism is not more evolved than polytheism. Not unless you think night is more evolved than day, because it comes after. If Doron's interested in religious history, he ought to know it's happened on a lot of worlds."

I laughed, but it was a faked laugh. I'd wanted her to bring up Doron's name, and now I was almost angry that she had. "What's happened on a lot of worlds—day and night?"

"Gods and God. People go along for a while worshiping a nice fat pantheon of deities, and then hard times hit and people want more reassurance. They get tired of coping with complexity; they want a machine or a parent to do it for them. They want to dump everything on one big Super Dooper so they can say, 'Never mind how bad everything is, Super Dooper is taking care of it.' So they're monotheists for a while."

"That doesn't sound like Doron," I said. I couldn't tell her I hadn't seen much reassurance in the *Manual*.

"Well, I'm giving you the curmudgeon's-eye view." She had sunk her chin into her neck so far, she was looking up at me through the gray fringe of her bangs. "I don't doubt Doron's a nice boy. Nice people make the best of whatever religion they're stuck with. They even generally think they're nice *because* of their religion. But sooner or later, even in a totalitarian monotheism, people start objecting to any Omnipotence that's willing to preside over a universe as nasty as this one."

"You think it's a nasty universe?" I said, struck to the heart. I wanted a nice universe, a fun universe, a playing-ball-and-floating-in-the-Mineral-Lake universe.

"You going Bimranite on me, Liss? Nicey-nicey? You going to say the parasites don't matter?—the torture, prisons, prejudices?—flagellation and self-flagellation?—humans and other animals eating each other alive?—firestorms, plagues, meteorites?—holy wars? If there's a Super Dooper, Super Dooper is not nice. So—" She shrugged. "After a while people decide it makes more sense to cope with complexity after all, and you get monotheism flaking away, with atheism moving in on one side and polytheism on the other. Day, night, day. I don't know if it'll ever stop rotating."

"Do you think—" I hesitated. "Do you think monotheism makes people judgmental?"

She lurched forward on her seat, aiming a forefinger at me. "You got it, girl! I don't know if it follows logically, but it sure as slud does in practice. When you think there's only one God, and you think your one God is always right, there's a big temptation to think there's only one right way of doing things. And if your God runs a universe where people get hurt, there's a big temptation to figure it's all right to hurt people—as long as they're people who don't agree with your one right way. Whereas if you've got a galaxy of assorted deities arguing about everything, you can take a more tolerant approach to disagreement." She hawked a laugh. "You talk about Bimranites needing Selection because they don't believe in souls, but it's not that simple."

"You mean they'd have Selection anyway?" Nothing is ever as simple as you thought it was, I knew that from experience. I suppose it's what keeps science going.

"Who knows?" Leona shrugged. "A lot of monotheists *have* believed in souls, and at least claimed to believe that their monogod took care of the rewards and punishments— all those heavens and hells you've heard about. But that hasn't stopped most of them from having their own version of Selection, officially or unofficially." She laughed, not a very jolly sound. "The unofficial ones are usually the worst."

I dreamed luscious dreams of rolling and romping with Doron, naked in the free-fall bliss of the Mineral Lake, naked in drifts of frozen limpet milk, so real that it was hard to believe I'd never been skin to skin with him. I woke and lay motionless in my sleep-swing, staring at darkness.

No. No. Leona was wrong. People weren't looking for a parent necessarily. They were looking for a system. They wanted the universe to make sense, even if that meant going to hell. Or Punishment. Everything made sense to Bimranites. That was one thing I envied them.

I hadn't expected to see Doron again very soon. But I was threading my loom in the Park only two days after that encounter at the spaceport when I looked up and there he was, standing beside the bench where I sat. I felt like a strummed filament. "Are you working?" I asked him. I was afraid of the answer, either way. But it wasn't anything I'd expected.

"No," he said. "I was taken off the case."

I began unthreading. "What does that mean?"

"It's somewhat unusual," he said. "The case was subsumed into a larger investigation. Would you mind if I sat down?"

"No, of course not."

He sat on the bench beside me—meaning on the other side of an armrest. "It's not 'of course,' " he said. "May I ask if—Would you like me to take back the *Manual*?"

"No, please don't, not unless you need it. I'm reading it. Well, bits and pieces of it." He looked infinitely vulnerable, a child at the top of a chute whose end was out of sight. Selectors must be held to higher standards. "Who was the man with the red beard?"

"One of my colleagues," he said. "It had to do with our work."

"Are you in trouble, Doron? Am I making trouble for you?"

He smiled a sad little quirk of a smile. "You're very kind, Liss. Thank you for that. No, I'm not in trouble. No, you're not making trouble for me." His lips tightened for an instant—shutting in what, I wondered. "I must have seemed very abrupt to you that day. It's just that we have to keep our work very separate from everything else."

"Yes, I know. I read that in the *Manual*." I smiled a real smile at him—he looked so dear—and instantly he blossomed into a real smile of his own.

"I was looking for you," he said, "because I wondered if you'd like to see the autumn flowerburst."

I laughed in sheer pleasure. "Yes, I'd like to see it. What is it?"

* * *

Flowerburst was spread across the hills just east of the city. Gravel paths (not only hard but lumpy) had been laid on some of the slopes, and people wandered along them, chatting and pointing. Children dashed and shouted and were scolded for stepping off the paths or trying to pick flowers. The smallest ones had to reach up to achieve that degree of naughtiness; most of the plants that bobbed their tempting blossoms on the wind were hip-high to an adult. Seen from the bottom of the slope, the hillside was like a wild mane of hair held by a tattered net, color flaunting and waving through the gray mesh of paths. Purple, orange, and red in manifold tints and shades, spattered with splotches of bright yellow, almost hid the gray-greens of the foliage. Irregular movements ran over the slopes—wind making the flower-heads fluff and shrug and stoop. Flying things buzzed or flitted or drifted among them—Bimran hoverbirds, anonymous multitudes of tinier creatures, and floating butterflies with wings like the powdered masks of Gantry Four. Breathing was like inhaling perfume, pungent and sweet. We strolled up a path between waving scarlet plumes.

"Did you know," Doron asked, "that butterflies are like humans—native to old Earth?"

"No, but I've seen them on a couple of other worlds. They're lovely."

"Yes," Doron said. "So lovely that people can't resist importing them. They've only been on Bimran for a few decades, but they're spreading fast. They're very popular."

I sneezed. "You'd better watch out," I said. "Butterflies can change your world."

"I know that," he said. "I've read the ecology things." He gave me one of those Dorony smiles that could be so many things at once—sober and tender and humorous. "We do try to be careful." His slim hand hovered beside a pair of damasked black and purple wings perched on the one golden blossom in a cluster of red. "I've thought of starshippers that way sometimes."

I laughed. The wings throbbed, swept downward, rose, and drifted away. "It sounds like a riddle: How is a starshipper like a butterfly?"

"Multicolored," he said. "Multicolored and flitting." He touched a tall, arching spray of red-orange. "I grow these," he said, "in my garden. I love them." Almost embarrassed at his own confession.

"So do the butterflies," I said.

"Yes. And even when the flowers are gone, the shape is beautiful. Of course, the butterflies are gone then, too."

We strolled our gravel track through the tumult of flowers. Two children ran past us, faces flushed, shouting with laughter. The wind patted me through my slimsuit. "May I ask you a question?" Doron said.

"Yes, do."

"Why did you—" he paused a moment, not exactly a hesitation— "change your sex?"

I laughed indignantly. "I didn't. It's your Migration Control that labeled me a man. I was born female and so far as I'm concerned I'll always be female."

"I'm sorry," he said. "I don't mean to offend you. I should have asked, 'Why did you have yourself sterilized?' "

"Because I didn't want to risk getting pregnant, and I don't like to bother with the temporary stuff."

"I see." His voice was very level. "Have you ever been married?"

"On the *Trojan* we didn't do that. I only know about it from history—and places like Bimran. No, I've never been married." I couldn't stop my mouth from shaping a smile. It was like hearing myself say, *No, I've never been circumcised. No, I've never danced around a maypole.* But dancing around a maypole might be fun.

"When you had yourself sterilized, were you expecting to be married?"

"No, of course not! I told you, Doron, we didn't do that."

"So you were anticipating sexual intercourse without marriage?"

I blinked at him. Interviewing technique category number three: direct pursuance. "Anticipating—? Yes, and without pregnancy, that's the whole idea. Of course, if I'd known what Bimran was like, I wouldn't have needed to bother, would I? Except it came in handy before Bimran. And if I hadn't bothered, I suppose I'd still be female by Bimran standards, and—" I stopped. "Do you mean to tell me," I said slowly, though he hadn't been telling me anything, "that if I were fertile, as you call it, I wouldn't be off limits to Bimran men?"

"If you were still female," he said, "you'd be a very— eligible woman, Liss."

"Eligible for what?" The only thing I could think of was Selection.

His turn to blink. "For marriage. I'm sure there would be many men courting you." A bleak and rueful little smile. "I wouldn't stand a chance."

"Oh, slud!" I stopped dead. Could I really have been so stupid, not to understand till now? Could Bimranites really be so stupid? Sarelli had all but told me; I just hadn't generalized it enough.

"Liss," Doron said quickly, before I could get it all integrated, "the point is not your status, or anyone else's. The point is what actions you choose to take in whatever status you have. You, I, anyone."

"Fine," I said. "I'll agree with that."

"And I take it you find some people sexually attractive?"

"Don't we all?"

"No, not everyone," he said seriously. "But most people do. Do you? You don't have to answer anything I'm asking. It's just—that I'm interested."

"Yes. I do find some people sexually attractive."

"And would you welcome sexual activity with such people?"

"Yes, I would."

"Even without marriage?"

"Yes."

"Even men?"

"Especially men."

We were facing each other straight, like partners or antagonists. Our voices were quiet. Anybody watching us would be seeing a calm, dispassionate discussion. "That would be fornication," Doron said. "And of course—I'm saying this because I'm not sure you've fully understood it yet, Liss—of course you could never marry a man. Any sexual activity between two men—for example, between you and me—is perversion, and perversion is fornication." A gust of perfume blew into my face.

≈ 14 ≈

Exactly because of the powerful feelings involved, sexual morality is a valid indicator of general morality. Any form of fornication is a sign of some deep flaw in the individual under observation.

—*From* Revised Manual for Selectors,
Working Draft, Chapter 11.

Nonsense? Of course it's nonsense!" Leona agreed. "What about it? Two thirds of what humans do has always been nonsense."

"But it's absurd!" I howled. I dropped onto her guest mushroom and rubbed my hands hard over my face.

She snorted—Leona's expression of sympathy. "Trying to change your spots?"

"It's absurd. Even if they want to outlaw homosexuality, it's absurd to apply it to me and Doron."

"No more absurd than making rules against homosexuality in the first place. Two people are sexually attracted to each other and can't get together because they're mutually taboo."

"But—but—"

"No, it's *not* more unfair because it's happening to you, Liss." She grunted and sighed, a double comment. "Listen, girl. Some societies used to claim that homosexuality was unnatural, but it's about as sure as anything gets that it evolved for good reason. Any group of hominids with a nice little proportion of nonreproducing homosexuals and a good solid core of bisexuals and heterosexuals had a better chance of survival. Eases the mating competition, helps keep people happy during birth spacing, more aunties and uncles to help support the kiddies, all that sort of thing. The same way family groups with plenty of healthy old folks tended to survive and reproduce better, so did the ones with a supply of nonbreeding young folks. You end up with positive selection for longevity and homosexuality—just not too much of either. Maybe Bimran hasn't heard about human evolution, but most of the species has. You're going to cry about it, are you?"

"I'm not sure, Leona. I thought I was laughing." I wiped my eyes. "Forget evolution. Sex is also a pretty good way of expressing affection."

She chuckled. "Not a bad one. Which is evolution, too. As soon as you've got a species that habitually uses sex to reinforce pair bonds—and that's what you get with brains so big the kids have to be born half-finished and it takes two parents to raise them—then you can bet it's going to reinforce some same-gender friendships too. The very people who enjoy a tumble with their mates are likely to enjoy a tumble with their best buddies."

"Not all of us," I said. "Some of us get stuck with radical heterosexuality. Irredeemable. And— Wait a minute, Leona." Implications were belatedly sinking in. "So I can't marry a man because I'm a man myself. Does that mean if I wanted to I could marry a woman?"

"You'd think so, wouldn't you? But the way Bimranites see it, the purpose of marriage is reproduction. Nobody gets married except reproductive pairs. It's all right to *stay* married after you've outlived your fertility, but only if you've had children. The way they see it—"

"Oh, slud! The toxic way they see it!"

Leona shrugged. "Don't blame me. You're the one who asked."

For a modest fee, you could get an artificial beard. I found that out when a hairdresser offered me one in the middle of a hairtrim. Better than a dermal graft, she told me, because you never had to shave.

"I don't think it's my style," I said.

"Quite a few of my customers decide on it when they reach change of sex. Especially the younger-looking ones. A beard clarifies the situation, you know. I've had people tell me it really does prevent embarrassing situations."

We were alone in her tiny shop. It was quiet except for the rhythmic hum of the combuster as she stroked it again and again over my hair. "That's short enough," I said, eyeing my image in the mirror screen. "Just shape it." On Bimran you didn't need to add, *very simply*.

"Of course it's the really young people, like you," the hairdresser pursued, "who appreciate that kind of help the most. I have one customer who turned out to be congenitally infertile." She stroked the combuster delicately around the edges of my face. "It was really tragic; they only found out at the premarital exam, and then of course the marriage had to be called off. She eventually decided on the beard—he, I mean—and he tells me it's made his life so much easier. And I think other people appreciate it too. Being able to tell by looking, you know. It's permanent, unless you want it removed. Genuine hair—choose your style and color—and it doesn't take any special care." She peered past my head, studying the screens. "This would look more masculine if I trimmed it right back at the temples."

"I don't want to look masculine," I said.

She straightened as if she'd been jerked by a string. "Oh."

It should have been simple. I was a starshipper. I knew about not fitting into somebody else's world. When you don't fit, you move on—that's not hard to figure out.

Except for two little things: I'd lost my starship, and I didn't want to go. There'd be another starship—one of these days, or months, or years—but it wouldn't be the *Trojan*. Starshippers are one big family in a lot of ways, far more uniform than the planetbound, and for good reason. Starships all do essentially the same thing, while planets (culturally speaking) fly off in all directions. And starships are a moving network; they communicate with each other—in port and between ports—more than they do with planets. But even so, starships aren't interchangeable. Some of them, at least compared to the *Trojan*, are stiff and regimented. Some of them are so keen on privacy and personal space that their crew members hardly talk to each other. And besides, I'd spent all my life on the *Trojan*; how could I know what transferring to another ship was really like? Suppose I didn't fit in? Suppose I left it for still another world, and didn't fit in there? You can get tired, very tired, of always being separate, always a resident alien. Maybe I was just losing my nerve, but I dreaded that.

And I realized now that from my first day on Bimran I'd been looking at this world in a different way from all the other worlds I'd seen, storing my data in a different kind of file—one marked *Life*, not *Memory*. On every other world, I'd been protected. When you're a starshipper, it doesn't matter how many clothes you take off; you're still wearing an impervious film of separation like an invisible bubblesuit. On Bimran—prissy, hands-off Bimran—I'd been naked and touching all the time. I was attached.

After flowerburst, the Bimran autumn turned gray. There were frosts for three nights running, and on the third morning a heavy fog that left a spiny fur of crystals on every twig and railing. When you touched them they crumbled. And when the fog cleared and the sun burned down from a flaring blue sky, they melted loose and fell in dryly whispering showers.

I didn't want to read the *Manual*. I didn't want to talk to Leona. I was still too bruised to see Doron, or Sarelli either. But I was sick of my own quarters. I started toward the spaceport, turned back, lost myself too briefly among sidestreets, and gravitated as always toward the Park. Clouds were moving in from the east—not the bright piled thunderheads of summer, but broad dark smears erasing the blue. Before I got to the Park the wind hit me like a shuttle's thruster blast, and then a cataract of rain. I dodged into the first open doorway.

It was a little library office, with a single row of consoles. Shray was just disconnecting from one of them. She hailed me with delight. "Nice day, Liss!"

Nice day, when the sky was falling. "Nice day," I said, and turned to fluff myself over the dryer at the entrance. Most shops on Bimran had these conveniences for the use of wet customers.

Shray stood beside me, looking out at the gush of falling water. "It's marvellous, isn't it?" she said.

I didn't say anything. The rain was impressive—I was probably more impressed than she was—but I didn't feel obliged to make conversation. I didn't want to be involved with these people. I had concerns of my own to think about.

She was willing to make the conversation without my help. "Morit enjoyed your discussion the other day. It's so stimulating to hear another viewpoint, don't you think?"

I tried a Leona-style grunt, but it needed practice. Shray gave me a sideways look.

"Of course," she said, "Morit always prefers to talk about God. I think that's rather anthropomorphic. Personally, I prefer to think in terms of the Oneness. But we're all speaking of the same thing. Clearly—"

"Or unclearly," I said.

She gurgled a laugh. "Oh, I like it! Clearly or unclearly, yes, there definitely is a Oneness. It's what underlies—or overlies—everything. Some of us call it God."

There it was again, the Bimranite *isn't it obvious?* attitude. Everything was obvious to Bimranites. "What makes you think everything's underlain?—or overlaid, or whatever? Why can't things just be the way they are?"

She blinked. "Well, of course, Liss, you must realize that the chances of the universe just—just happening are absolutely infinitesimal."

"What do you mean by the universe?"

She fluttered her fingers vaguely. "All this. The stars . . . the planets . . . life . . . human beings . . ."

"You mean the way things are?"

She laughed her sunny laugh. "Yes, the way things are. You have such a nice way of putting things, Liss."

"Thanks."

"You do see what I mean, don't you? It's infinitely unlikely that everything would have come together just this way without a guiding power to direct it."

"So?" I said. As far as I could see, she was telling me that water is wet. Which it certainly was on Bimran. I stared at the plunging rain. A crack of thunder like a splitting world made me jerk.

"So?" Shray repeated. She looked baffled. "Well, everything *has* come together just this way. There *must* have been a guiding power."

"Uh—why?"

She made helpless motions. "Well, I just said! Don't you see? If you leave everything to chance, it's so improbable it just wouldn't happen."

I sighed impatiently. "What wouldn't happen?"

If I was impatient, Shray was exasperated—or as exasperated as a Bimranite was likely to get. "Well, the universe! The way things are!"

I hit the threshold of understanding. Amazing how often sheer repetition will do it. "Oh! You're assuming this is how your Guiding Power *meant* for things to be."

"Yes," she said uncertainly. "That is, no, I'm not assuming anything, it just follows logically. The Creator *must* have intended this universe, or nothing so unlikely would have happened."

I couldn't help it, I burst out laughing. Shray joined in hesitantly. I wiped my eyes. "But *something* would have happened, Shray."

"Yes? I don't follow."

"If you spin a million-sided die," I said (I'd played with those simulations on Gantry Four) "the odds are one in a million that the side I bet on will come up. But the odds are a million in a million, otherwise known as a sure thing, that *some* side will come up. If it hadn't been this universe it would have been another. And very likely there'd be critters of some kind sitting on a lump of gravity waves, drinking boiled anti-mesons and saying, 'This couldn't have happened by chance, the Creator must have planned it.'"

"Oh, you're wrong, Liss! I understand that the conditions for the development of intelligent life are *very* improbable. That's really the whole point, isn't it?"

"I didn't think so," I said, a little dazedly. "I thought we were asking whether the universe could have occurred without preplanning."

"And we see that it can't," Shray said positively. "It's too improbable."

"*This* universe is improbable," I said. "And so is every other universe. Every side of the die is improbable, but one of them always comes up. All you're saying is, 'If things weren't exactly the way they are, they'd be different.' I definitely agree with that."

She smiled uncertainly. "Well, then. We do agree, after all."

"You might say so." At least the rain was letting up. People were venturing onto the street again, laughing at their own wetness, dull Bimran clothes brightened by the pearling water. On the far side of the street, a slender person in black walked soberly through the drizzle. Not Doron, but Doronlike. I turned to Shray. "Are you afraid of Selection?"

Her eyes widened. That was too abrupt. For seconds she only stared at me, lost for anything to say. "Why, no. Not afraid. Of course not." She perked up. "You know the saying—or, I'm sorry, perhaps you don't—'Take care of your neighbors and Selection will take care of itself.' One tries to be a good person, and then there's no cause for worry."

"Shouldn't anybody who attends Vailid's meetings and collects offworld money for her be worried?"

She glanced around the library with little scuttling movements of her eyes. "Vailid has a visitor's permit. Bimran is perfectly free, you know."

"Then why do you want so much to change it?" I lifted my hand. "No, don't answer that. But if I were you I'd watch out. People are getting investigated."

She laughed brightly. "Well, it's been nice talking to you, Liss. I do hope I'll see you again soon. I must go now."

I watched her bobbing along through the drizzle. All right, I'd tried to warn her. I just wasn't sure what I was warning her of.

One thing I was sure about: I wouldn't leave Bimran without seeing Doron again. We'd left too much unfinished.

So I went looking for him—what were a few bruises more or less?—and instead I found Sarelli. I saw his fingers begin to dance before we were within speaking distance. That looked different to me now, itchy and sticky.

"You missed a lesson, Rainbow Man. Losing interest?"

Anger surged up in me, and I saw his eyes widen speculatively. I wasn't controlling blood flow, I wasn't monitoring my breath. "I don't want a lesson," I said. "And I don't want to play games, Sarelli. What would you do if I weren't a man?"

He hung perfectly still, eyebrows and fingers frozen in the moment's arch. It was so quiet I could hear the watch in my ear purring off the seconds. Then the trajectories resumed, but slowly, his fingers caressing air, his brows drawing together in what on any other face I would have called a look of sadness. "I wouldn't call you Rainbow Man, would I?"

I burst into an angry laugh. "Slud, Sarelli!"

But he was past that dangerous moment when he might have exposed himself. " 'What if things had been different?'

is a question that can't be honestly answered—except with
'I don't know.' I don't know, Rainbow Man. Is there any
point in asking?"

"I thought there was. I want to know if staying on Bimran
is worth the pain."

Not a flicker of surprise. "Aren't you lucky to have the
option?" A little twist of smile or sneer. "Do you expect
advice from me, Rainbow Man?"

"Don't call me that!"

He reared his head backward, studying me from as far
away as possible without actually ceding ground. "We know
what you are, Liss," he said gravely. "And the time line runs
only one way."

He meant I couldn't go back to being what I'd been. But
I was a starshipper; his words were heavier to me than to
him. Ever since qualate physics separated gravitational mass
from inertial mass, it's only time dilation that makes light
speed a limit. Regardless of what Vailid's friends seemed to
think, you can't get faster than instantaneous. If you could
ride a photon with old man Einstein, you'd be everywhere
you were going at once, and never mind that the people on
your route were clocking you at a steady two-hundred-nine-
ty-nine-thousand-plus kilometers per second. The slud gets
you so close to a photon's viewpoint—and yet so unbridge-
ably far from it—that the places you can't go back to don't
even exist. I didn't want that to happen to Bimran, I just
didn't want it. "There's such a thing as regeneration," I said.
"How far do your techniques go, Sarelli?"

"Tissue repair," he said. "Not organ regrowth." He stood
very quietly, his hands still again. "That's the most you'll
find on Bimran. If that can help, I'll help you, Liss."

I let out a breath I must have been holding since my last

question. I'd need new ovaries . . . new fallopian tubes . . . I wasn't sure what else. "Transplants?" I said.

He shook his head slowly. "On Ishi Three," he said. "For a very steep price. Six years Galactic round-trip, if you can hitch a ride both ways on a starship."

"And nobody I know would be alive when I got back here," I said. "And at shuttle speeds it would take me— what, ten years?—and I'd be back in time to help you take care of your grandchildren. No, thanks."

He watched me a moment more before he nodded. "So, Rainbow Man." It sounded deliberate, but I didn't hear any mockery in it. "Is it worth it?"

"I'll stay on Bimran," I said. "I don't know if it's worth it, Sarelli, I don't know what's worth what. But I know I want to stay, so I'm staying."

His face lit, and he tossed back his head in a crow of exuberant laughter. "Come for a footboard run with me?" he challenged. "Out past Northtown? I'll show you something."

≈ 15 ≈

A reward given privately for past good deeds is an expense that benefits one individual. A public, long-lasting reward is an investment in future good deeds and thus can benefit the world.

—*From* Revised Manual for Selectors,
Working Draft, Chapter 8.

Yes, show me!" Footboard run? I could have raised my arms and soared—or at least I felt like it. Decision taken and applied. Whatever was working itself out between Doron and me would work itself out on Bimran, with all the time it needed. And meanwhile I could play games with Sarelli, play like a child. I lifted my arms, trailing the blue-green streamers of my sleeves, and remembered the constraints of reality. "Oh—but my footboard's died."

"I have a spare one you could use," Sarelli said. "My place is on the way."

This was new. I'd never even learned what part of town Sarelli lived in, much less been invited there. "Let's go, then."

As it turned out, he lived in Riverside—the labyrinth of five- and six-decked buildings, tied together by enclosed skywalks like colored ribbons, that separated the Park from the river. "How do you find your way home?" I asked Sarelli. "They all look alike."

"How do you find your way home on board a starship? They're all different. Look."

Bimran walls, like Bimran pavements, were generally hard and unyielding. If you bumped into one, it hurt. The walls of Sarelli's neighborhood were the colors of Bimran dirt: reddish shades of brown, yellowish shades of brown. (On an agricultural planet like Bimran, dirt is very important.) Some building façades were all one tone, some shaded gradually from one to another, some were patterned with swirling streaks or checkered grids. Variety in monotony. But he was right about the resemblance to starship life. Planetbound visitors on shipboard—customs officials, local dignitaries, potential customers—are likely to say things like "How do you find your way around? It's a labyrinth." On the *Trojan* we always thought they were pretty dense for not noticing the guidelines. On the *Trojan* you were never lost.

So I started scanning the buildings for directional markers of some kind. "The farther from the Park, the more colors?" I hazarded.

Sarelli grinned. "The closer to the river, the more *distinct* the colors. And the farther downstream, the more textured the surface. Simple enough?"

"And *you* live—let me guess—in the most distinct and the most textured corner. Right?"

He tossed back his head to laugh. "Bravo, Liss! And here we are. Would you rather wait in the lobby or outside?"

Before I could say "Huh?" he had slid open a door and slipped into the building. But he held the door open with one hand and grinned at me. I followed him in. The lobby was nothing but a wide corridor with scattered seats—the usual Bimran mushrooms—and widely spaced doors on both sides. A few people were sitting farther along it, each alone. The ceiling was painted with tree fronds and butterflies.

I turned to Sarelli. "You're telling me that private quarters are private? You're not going to invite me in?"

"It wouldn't look right, would it?" His voice was barely mocking, just enough to make it uncertain whether he was speaking his own mind or sardonically quoting someone else's. "I'll be back in two minutes." He turned away and keyed the first door on the right. I got a glimpse of a large uncluttered room, all chaste browns and ambers, as the door opened and closed behind him.

I could think of a couple of reasons why Bimranites might be so protective of their privacy. Most of Bimran life was thoroughly public, and having your own quarters to yourself could be an antidote. Or it could be part of the same phenomenon. Bimranites didn't do things without impartial witnesses. It wouldn't look right.

I got another glimpse as Sarelli whisked out again, well within his two minutes, riding one footboard and carrying another. He presented it to me with a flourish. "Freedom," he said. "All I can give you, Liss."

I'd never been very far north before. We skimmed along the Riverside streets, crossing bridges now and then to look at something on the other side—a butterfly store, a children's playground full of slanting tree trunks and swinging vines, Sarelli's school. A school, on Bimran, was a public building where anybody was welcome to give lessons on any subject they could find students for. Classes, times, and fees were posted on a notice board at the main entrance. There was also a sign-up board for building maintenance volunteers. Very much a do-it-yourself operation. "It's a lot like the *Trojan*," I said.

Sarelli ran his long fingers caressingly around the curve of the notice board. "Is it? Can a starshipper think that Bimran resembles a starship?"

"Only bits of it," I said. "Can a Bimranite think so?"

"Bits of a Bimranite, perhaps."

We raced. We played tag and composed nonsense rhymes and sang songs from worlds I'd seen and Sarelli hadn't. In this gravity, my flowsuit's extensible streamers fluttered and snapped a good two meters behind me at top speed. At an intersection we sailed through a wedding—another form of public entertainment on Bimran—just as the jeweler activated the rings and the happy couple raised their hands with a flash of light. We wove through the crowd of wedding guests and onlookers without slowing. Everybody stared. Someone hailed me exuberantly, "Rainbow Man!" Sarelli was eating it up, his grin as bright as the glints from his clothes. It seemed to me that Sarelli in his glittering dark brown was just as odd as I was, but he didn't get the same reaction.

We slowed down to facilitate communication; shouting gets monotonous. "Rainbow Man!" a chorus of voices called from a passing floatcar.

"Ever been out with a famous person before?" I asked Sarelli.

"Ever been famous before?" he retorted.

"No."

"And no."

We laughed. "What's over there?" I pointed across the river, where I could see an open space like a little park, with a few scrawny trees, at least one of which seemed to be dead, and a loose crowd of people milling slowly or sitting on what looked like bare ground.

"We're in Northtown," Sarelli said, which wasn't exactly an answer. His grin had disappeared. He accelerated away from me, and I had to hit top speed for a minute to catch up.

It was true the look and smell of the city were different

here. The street we cruised along was passably normal: well maintained, with luminous strips down the edges of the pavement, and plants in containers hung from cables between buildings. But definitely not as clean as a Southtown street. Nor—though we passed a team of determined-looking young people repairing a section of roadway—quite as well maintained. There were cracks in the paving, some of the plants were shriveled and ragged, and in places the luminous strips seemed to have been torn or scraped away. There was a fair amount of traffic, but it was different. The floatcars hissed along at an unsociable speed, closed like spacecraft. People on foot or footboard watched each other furtively. Nobody here was calling me "Rainbow Man." And across the river, and down sidestreets on this side, the look was still shabbier and seedier. "Who takes care of the streets around here?" I asked Sarelli. "And drainage, power supply, things like that?"

He shifted on his footboard to face me, offering his back to the rest of the street and leading with his shoulder. "In Northtown? Mostly volunteers from elsewhere," he said. "It's a good way to demonstrate virtue." He shot out a hand to touch the leafless stems of a vine that trailed from the projecting upper deck of a building. "I bring a class out here every year to unclog the water outlets. Morality without water isn't as easy as some people seem to think. We arrange the plants as indicators; they draw water off the same tubing as the residents do. And every time we come, most of the outlets are clogged again." He spun away from me, circled a dark spot on the pavement that looked more like stain than decoration, and fell into pace beside me again. "Somebody killed somebody there," he said.

"Literally there? Literally killed?" I looked back at the stain through my fluttering streamers.

"Literally literally." He laughed. "No crime on Bimran doesn't mean we don't have the occasional murder."

We were coming to the edge of the city—an abrupt edge, not like the trailing-off at the far side of Southtown, where buildings thinned out gradually and then clustered again at the spaceport. Now there was no more foot traffic, except Sarelli and me. The last dingy buildings clumped together like dirty crystals. I put on a burst of speed.

Ahead, the road forked, one branch sticking to the river shore while the other turned right to lose itself among climbing hills. Just before the fork, a low block of buildings, Bimran-sunlight yellow, sat within a lower wall along the river bank, its neatness looking out of place. "Where are we going?" I called back to Sarelli.

He drifted slowly after me, his head tilted back a little, his smile savoring. I waited for him. "A sea-blue comet," he said, and lifted his hand through the streamers that were just settling around me, tossing them high. Without stopping (like a dancer, Sarelli could always make two gestures out of one, or one out of two) his hand moved on to point. "There, Rainbow Man. Comet Man. Shooting Star." His eyes were on me, but his five fingers pointed stiffly toward the yellow compound of buildings.

I turned to look, curious. "What is it?"

He was rocking his footboard, dancing, teasing. "You don't know? You really don't know? I told you once I'd bring you here someday. Race you to the door?"

"You're on!" I got a moment's start on him, but he closed the gap quickly, and we whizzed side by side down the road. I couldn't see a door. The outer wall was no more than waist high, and featureless: a simple statement of boundary. Behind the wall, there was one long square-cornered box of a building that looked just as blank, with smaller boxes around it. Everything was the same indiscriminately warm yellow, textured just enough not to be shiny.

A large floatcar passed us, whipping my streamers into Sarelli's face, and turned through a gap in the yellow wall. We followed, Sarelli gaining on the turn.

A wide area in front of the main building was paved in a deeper tone of the same yellow, and a few vehicles were already parked there. People were getting out of the floatcar. Sarelli made a feint of swerving around them and then cut through the group like a jet of dark flame, outdistancing me in a second. He waited, grinning, exchanging greetings with the floatcar passengers, while I let them crowd through the doorway ahead of me. The doorway itself was an unadorned opening in the building's blank front, with no sign that it ever was or could be closed, and just wide enough for Sarelli and me to enter together.

Inside, a blank-walled corridor led left and right. From the looks of it, it must run the whole length of the building's front. The walls stretched unbroken and undecorated. The group that had just come in were walking silently down the left leg of the corridor. Down the right and farther away, I could see a few other people, also going away from us.

"Which way?" Sarelli asked me, jigging his footboard left and right. He was giving me the look a cargo sample gets from a customs inspector, and at that moment I wouldn't have asked a question if my life depended on it. Well, maybe my life, but not my next meal.

"Right," I said, and turned without hesitation.

We cruised down the corridor. The people ahead of us disappeared around what was apparently the far corner. I pictured one endless corridor all the way around the building, with people who went left running into people who went right on the other side, and no way into whatever was hiding in the middle. I found that I was setting the pace. Every time I speeded up or slowed down a little, Sarelli stayed beside me. He was gazing straight ahead now, and his face had settled into a bland mask that was very un-Sarellian.

The ninety-degree bend in the corridor wasn't actually at the extreme corner of the building. The only way you could tell that, without measuring, was from the row of viewports on the right wall, opening on a range of snug little rooms, side by side and all alike, except for the colors. The first one was all in shades of pink, like quartz with different concentrations of titanium; palest pink walls and ceiling, dotted here and there with pinker butterflies and rosettes of flowers, a vivid pink coverlet sprinkled with white, and a soft pouf of pink around the sleeping face. I stared, and my footboard carried me past before I remembered I had the power to stop it.

By that time I was looking into the next viewport; they were only a few decimeters apart. This one was in lavenders and violets, and the face nestled in the pillow was very beautiful. I stopped.

The flowers on the coverlet and walls (there were no butterflies this time) might be artificial or preserved, but the figure in the bed looked very convincingly alive and human. Only the face showed. Everything else—body, hands, hair— was hidden under the dainty coverings and wraps. But the nostrils moved ever so slightly with gentle breath, the eyelids quivered, little smiles played over the lips. It was an old face, but a sweet one, and it wore an expression of utter contentment.

"If you watch long enough," Sarelli said mildly, "you'll see her laugh."

"Who is she?"

Sarelli pursed his lips. "It doesn't matter. You can buy a guidebook downtown if you're really curious."

"What's she doing here?"

He studied me, very much a teacher's expression. "What does it look like she's doing?"

I watched another smile flicker across the sweet old lips. "Enjoying herself. Having a very good dream after a very good day."

"Exactly," Sarelli said. "After a very good life, in fact. Not necessarily an easy one—notice the lines around the lips— but not an excessively difficult one, either."

"How do you know?"

He smiled a Sarelli smile. "How do we know anything? I judge on the basis of the available evidence, which is always incomplete. Do you want to see more?"

I didn't answer. I toed my footboard very thoughtfully, and we drifted slowly down the line. They were all alike and all different—different color schemes and decorations, different faces, many of them clearly elderly, others apparently midlife, a few startlingly young, almost children. I saw one laughing, eyes still closed. "Or is he crying?" I asked Sarelli. Without the sound, it was hard to tell.

"No, it's a laugh," he answered me. "Look at the cheek muscles and the eyes. There! See that?"

I took his word for it. I wanted to take his word for it. But I could see for myself the more obvious and more common signs of pleasure: smiles, heads gently rolling as they snuggled more cozily into the pretty pillows, lips throbbing with what must have sounded like a purr of contentment or a sigh of ecstasy.

The farther we got into the building, the more often we saw other observers—staring, like us, through the viewports;

like us, talking a little but not much. I hardly noticed when we came to another turn, and another and another, except that sometimes the viewports were on the right and sometimes on the left. People had come in groups, in families, in couples, or alone. There weren't many footboards—most people would have come by floatcar—and slow as our pace was, it was faster than many others. Some walked steadily, others stood motionless before a viewport. There were children of all sizes, most with adults, but some in whispering, giggling crowds of their own kind, embarrassed and trying to be unimpressed.

Some of the observers really did have guidebooks and consulted them frequently, pointing out particular sleepers to each other and reading passages aloud. ". . . For sixteen years, volunteered an average of four hours per day at the Northtown Medical Center, while caring for her own family and her deceased brother's . . . founder of the Sewer Maintenance Club of Riverside and an active member of three local tree-care groups . . . known to all his students as a friend and counselor. . . ."

"What do you call this place?" I asked Sarelli at last. My lips had gotten so dry they stuck together.

"The Selection Center."

"And this is Bliss?"

"This is Bliss," he said gravely.

"Then where's Punishment?"

He took my arm. I wasn't used to being touched anymore, and it startled me. But his tense fingers were very businesslike, gripping my upper arm as if he expected me to try to get away. He steered me around another corner, along another corridor, this one without viewports, and through a narrower opening into a chillier space. Then he let go. "Hear it, Rainbow Man?"

I heard it. We had passed through some unseen curtain, and on this side the air was full of noises, noises I didn't know how to identify. I pressed down my heel and glided away from Sarelli, looking for viewports in the blank yellow walls. But it was a very short corridor. I had to go around another corner before I heard them.

Viewport after viewport, looking not into separate tiny rooms but into one narrow hall, where bodies lay strewn on a long table. They were naked except for the straps that held them down and the catheters and wires that infiltrated them. They were alive. And in this corridor there was no acoustic barrier. I could hear the noises they made.

I was shaking when we came back at last into the long blank lobby, and my footboard seemed to have developed a will of its own. I had to get off to keep it from zigzagging into walls. I faced Sarelli as if he were my worst enemy. "What did they do?" I demanded.

He eased away from me a little, his head tilted back and his eyebrows arching, as if every feature of him were trying to escape. "They broke the Commandments," he said. "It's very simple. They broke the Commandments."

"Your stinking simple toxic little four commandments? Are they *that* important?" I hadn't spoken, hadn't tried to speak, while we were in there, hadn't looked at him. Ordinary human communication would have been a kind of sacrilege, like yawning in the face of agony. My voice was too loud now, and shaking. I had a vague awareness that there were other people in the corridor, coming or going, keeping well away from Sarelli and me.

"You don't understand the principle, do you?" Sarelli said quietly. "Didn't I tell you it doesn't matter what the Commandments are? Yes, they're that important, Liss—exactly *that* important." He pointed back the way we had come, his whole long arm stretched level at shoulder height. "Do you know why? Because they exist. Because if you break one, you're defying God."

"No God is doing that." I jerked a quick finger in the direction he had pointed. "It's people doing it to people. Who thought up this system? Who does it to you?"

Sarelli stooped to pick up his own footboard, then mine. We moved slowly toward the entrance. "People need rules, Liss. They get sloppy without a framework. People need to be taught. They need incentives. Northtown is what's left of what used to be planetwide problems."

"You mean you've segregated the people you don't want to eat dinner with."

He stopped. "Don't tell me what I mean, Liss," he said evenly. "I live here. I don't have your option of leaving. And I eat dinner in Northtown as often as I dine with you, though it's less pleasant. Nobody's segregated. The people who live in Northtown have precipitated out of the rest of Bimran. And the Northtown population isn't growing. We like to think it's shrinking, which may even be true. Most of the people selected for Punishment come from Northtown now, though not all. By no means all." He set down our footboards. "You like to ask questions, Rainbow Man. Why don't you ask what's caused the addicts and the violent and the lecherous and the avaricious and the destructive to leave their homes and congregate in Northtown?"

"All right, tell me why."

"Because," he said, "normal Bimran society no longer tolerates that kind of behavior. They had to come to Northtown to find suppliers and customers and victims."

"You mean," I said, "that normal Bimran society is terri-

fied of ending up on the table back there." I almost choked
on it.

"Don't tell me what I mean." He stepped onto his board.
Maybe it was the little added height, or maybe something in
his posture, that gave him back the Sarellian jauntiness I
hadn't noticed him losing. "Selection is the framework," he
said. "It isn't always enough to know what God commands."
He rocked his footboard, edging toward me and away, toward and away again. "It helps if you can see visible consequences. Object lessons." He spun the board and cruised
toward the entrance.

In the doorway itself he waited for me, a conspicuous
bright brown beacon. I had to stand aside to let a group of
more than a dozen middle-aged people enter. Sarelli followed them with his eyes. "A popular place," I said bitterly.

"We come here," Sarelli said, "to see our future. It's part
of being Bimranite."

The little buildings outside the main building were no
more than cubicles four or five meters on a side, but each
one was set in its own little garden. I had thought they were
as blank-faced as the main building; but that was only on the
side toward the compound's low outer wall. Elsewhere there
were viewports looking out on the fringe of garden that
separated them from the main building and from each other.
There were doorways, and paths, and people on the paths
and going in and out of doors, closing them carefully behind
them. They all wore black. *Selector holes,* I thought with a
sudden burst of scorn. This was where Selectors came to
compose their reports, or maybe just to be near the results
of their handiwork. I sped up, heading for the gap in the wall
as if it were an airlock starting to close, and in the gap itself
I almost knocked into Doron.

We both stopped. Sarelli slid into place beside me.

"Nice day," Doron said. He looked stricken.

I couldn't answer. "Nice day," Sarelli said.

I could see the orange snout of a sourfruit peeking out of Doron's shoulder carry. Very homey, very domestic. It made me ask the stupid question whose answer I suddenly knew. "What are you doing here?"

"I live here," he said. He had gotten his face under control to match his voice.

"Nice day," I said, and shoved past him.

Sarelli caught up a few seconds later, and we sped back toward the city without a word. Northtown had a reason to be dreary. Who would want to live close to that horror if they could afford to move elsewhere? Answer: Selectors, that's who.

"Let's go eat something very intoxicating," I said. "I want to get the taste of 'Nice day' out of my mouth."

≋ 16 ≋

Selectors will travel wherever needed and stay as long as their duties require, but their place of residence will be always and exclusively the Selection Center. It is important for each Selector to live alone and in total privacy. Privacy is the Selector's refuge.
> —*From* Revised Manual for Selectors,
> Working Draft, Chapter 1.

Leona came to see me the next morning. On Bimran, if somebody came to your door you had to get up and open it yourself. She walked right in and sank herself into a mushroom. "I saw you come in yesterday, Liss, but I sure as slud wasn't brave enough to tangle with you then. What happened to you?"

"The problem is," I said, "there's no way to get smashed on this planet. I need a good withdrawal syndrome."

She gave me a hard look. "If you spend enough time in Northtown, you'll find ways. But not as long as you stick with people who have something to lose. It's the ones already in hell that don't mind getting themselves damned."

I picked up a pot of yellow Bimran flowers and threw it against the hard Bimran wall. It shattered nicely, making a satisfactory mess of broken stems and scattered dirt on the floor.

Leona bellowed with laughter. "Good girl! I haven't seen

an honest tantrum in ten years Galactic. Now are you going to tell me what happened?"

I poked at the broken pot with my toe. It was too bad about the flowers. But I could plant the pieces and see what grew back. "I saw the Selection Center," I said.

Leona's face suddenly became a lot older. "Right," she said flatly, and slapped her hands down on her thighs. "Well, that's it. You knew it before, but now you *know* it. Or now you know what it is you thought you knew. You leaving Bimran?"

"I don't know," I said, kneeling to sort out the broken plant from the shards and dirt. Yesterday it had seemed so simple, my decision to stay had been so final, and now I found out I hadn't decided anything at all. "I'm thinking about it." I couldn't look at her while I said that. If I left Bimran on a starship, Leona would be dead before I had time to make a new friend. But so would the people on the Selection Center tables. It was a way of wiping them out, a *coup de grace*. Only not for them. My running to the stars wouldn't take one nanosecond off their agony. It would merely let me tell myself it was all over.

And it would be. The pain would all end eventually, and why shouldn't I project myself into that future? Why should I stay here and now, knowing every moment of every day and night what was going on at the north end of town?

"You're getting your hands dirty, messing around down there," Leona said, "and I don't think you're doing the flowers much good. I went through the same thing, you know."

I stopped fiddling in the dirt and looked up at her. "Does that make it all right?"

She snorted. "I just mean there's no hurry. You can only hurry one way."

She didn't need to say any more than that. *There's no round-trip* is a starship proverb. If I left today, there'd be no use changing my mind tomorrow. But if I stayed, I could change my mind anytime I wanted; it would never be too late.

"How long—" I swallowed and started again. "How long does Punishment last?"

Leona grimaced. "Depends on what shape a person's in to start with. They keep them alive as long as possible. It averages forty, fifty years—that's according to Korlo's cousin who works out there as a technician." She looked at me hard. "You don't change a world by leaving it, Liss. Whether you stay or not, you've still got to get used to the idea of the Selection Center. You don't have to like it, you just have to know it's there. And if somebody hurts, it doesn't matter if you call it past or present or future. Hurt is hurt."

I didn't make any more decisions. Two days later I was still going through the motions of my normal Bimran routines, selling a gold fluffball for a footboard and enough currency to feed me a few more days, and when I looked up from counting the money, there was Doron within arm's reach.

"Will you have a drink with me, Liss?" He didn't know the answer to that question; it showed in his eyes and his voice.

Neither did I, until I tucked my chin down in the Bimranite silent *yes*. I stuck the footboard into my shoulder carry, and we crossed a mossy space to the little drinkshop where he had probably been waiting. He didn't speak again until we were sitting opposite each other across a narrow slab of table, each with a cup of something sweet and sour.

"I'm glad you were there," he said. "I wanted you to see it. That is, I knew you had to see it. But I—" he looked down at his cup— "I was putting it off. I thought the *Manual*—" his voice rasped for a moment, as if his throat were dry to roughness— "could be a substitute."

I took a drink. I didn't have anything to say.

"Every Selector," Doron said, "is required to live at the Center. Each of us has a private residence there." He smiled faintly. " 'Residence' is the proper term, but we call them 'boxes.' "

"I saw them," I said. I took another drink. "I saw your Bliss and your Punishment."

"I know," he said.

"Are visitors observed while they watch?"

"Yes," he said. "There are records made."

"Your Center must be an expensive operation," I said. "Who pays for it?"

"It's mostly contributions," Doron said. "Materials and supplies are all contributed. What we can't use directly we sell. Selectors," he added, "pay all their own expenses, except housing and necessary transportation. In fact, we're forbidden to accept gifts. You may have read that in the *Manual*."

"I really haven't read much of it. How does a Selector pay for things?"

He smiled wanly. I must have sounded hostile. "Like other people. We get a small stipend from the Center, enough to cover basic food. And often we take temporary jobs, wherever we happen to be working."

"Doesn't that interfere with your, ah, work?"

"Oh, no," he said. "It helps." He ran one fingertip along the rim of his cup. "Thank you for talking to me. You're the first offworlder I've ever really known. I'm—interested in your responses. You teach me a lot."

"About what?"

"About Bimran. About myself." He looked down again, and up again to meet my eyes. "I'm afraid I'm very selfish. I hope what you saw at the Center won't drive you away from Bimran."

"Tell me one thing," I said. "Do you ever watch them?"

"Sometimes."

"Including the ones you've Selected?"

"Always." He watched me desolately. A lonely business, Selection.

"I just bought a new footboard," I said. "Would you like to take a run out to the hills?"

We tooled through the streets of the city without a word. Doron wasn't as adept on a footboard as Sarelli, but he kept beside me as I pushed up to top speed. Top speed was pretty slow, actually, though it did make a strong enough wind to rip away some of the tension. But it barely roughened the surface of the pain I seemed to be carrying underneath. We passed the road that ran up to the ski slopes where we'd first drunk limpet milk together, and turned up another that lost itself behind the path-netted hillside where we had argued in the midst of flowerburst. I swerved onto a path, spewing gravel, and knew in a few seconds that I had lost Doron. I slowed to a stop.

He came walking up the path, his board under his arm. "Footboards damage the paths," he said.

I joggled my board to and fro like Sarelli, between potential explosions—of anger or of laughter. But I didn't explode. I stepped off and stowed my footboard in my shoulder carry. "And it wouldn't look right, would it," I said, "for a Selector to be messing up the paths?"

He smiled faintly. "These paths give a lot of pleasure to a lot of people."

My potential explosions deactivated, all that energy trans-
forming into a little lump of unidentified matter in my chest.
I'd known plenty of people—myself, for example—so concerned about making their own statements they never gave
a thought to who was going to rake the gravel back onto the
path. When it came right down to it, I liked Doron's way
better.

We walked uphill into a raw breeze, almost as sharp as the
one we'd generated. "There are roughly seven million people on Bimran," Doron said.

"I know."

"On the average, about ten people per year are Selected."

"I see," I said. I had wanted to be with him, I had thought
we could be friends again—friends or whatever we were—
but the hard lump in my chest seemed to be pulling me out
of shape, twisting me away from him. *I don't fit here. Anywhere.*

"I don't know," I said, "why I wanted to come here." I
noticed we had stopped. The bleak gray fields bristled with
dry stalks. A few weeks ago this had been butterfly pasture,
a harvest of blowing color. Now there was frost on the
seedheads.

"Here's a place," Doron said. "We could sit down." He
took a step off the path, where a patch of moss broke the
forest of bare stems.

"Wouldn't look right, would it? Aren't we supposed to
stay on the paths?"

"Only to protect the flowers. If we don't break any plants
that are still setting seeds, it's all right."

"Do nothing you know to be harmful," I said, quoting the
Manual. I sat down on the moss, and he sat beside me,
crossing his legs—a useful posture for holding himself separate at close range.

"I should have taken you there myself," he said. No question about the meaning of *there*.

I spread my fingers—a negative gesture on the *Trojan*—and then remembered to shake my head. "It's all right. I mean it's all right you didn't take me. What I saw wasn't all right."

"You do understand," he said—not a question— "that from my point of view it *is* all right."

"I understand that. I understand why. You've explained it to me." I picked at the little silver tassels on my sleeve. "I've been a marvellous hypocrite, Doron. You've explained it, I've read the *Manual*—well, I've read a little of the *Manual*—I understand the principle. I didn't learn anything new at the Selection Center. So why am I behaving as if I'd just had this great revelation?"

He waited a moment—making sure I'd phased out—before he said mildly, "That's why there has to be a Selection Center."

I yelped a laugh. "To offend offworlders?"

"It wasn't built for offworlders," he said. "Knowing principles isn't enough. People need to see reality."

That was more or less what Sarelli had said. Everything made sense to Bimranites. The flowerstalks rattled in the wind, and a long shudder went through me and exited. "You're cold," Doron said, his voice almost breaking on it, as if he were talking about somebody with an incurable wound.

"Yes." But it wasn't the wind that hurt, it was the not fitting. Without even leaning, I could have laid my hands on his thighs, and we would still have been light-years apart. "Doron—"

"I could tell you," he said, "the kinds of crimes those

people on the table have committed, the kind of lives they've led, the kinds of damage they've done to other people. But you know those things, if you've read the *Manual*. You know the things we look for."

"Yes. Yes." I had to clench my jaw between words to keep my teeth from chattering. But the lump inside me was blooming into heat, the crudest form of energy. "I know these things, Doron. I know that according to your toxic *Manual* homosexuality is fornication, and fornication is sin. I know that technically—that's the *Manual*'s technicalities, nobody else's—that's what it would be if we had sex together—homosexuality and fornication and sin. But humanly, Doron—and we *are* human, both of us, we're members of the same species—tell me what in the universe would be wrong with me kissing you right now?"

"You're a man," he said seriously. "I can't marry you."

I couldn't help it; I exploded into laughter. "And you never kiss anybody you can't marry?" I said, when I could get the words out.

He hadn't altered his expression, just waited for my outburst to finish. "Where the possibility of marriage does not exist," he said evenly, "a sexual kiss is an invitation to fornication. And regardless of that, any sexual kiss between men is a perversion—which under the *Manual*'s guidelines is a form of fornication."

Doron was Doron; he could always meet a stare without flinching. "You don't," I said, "you can't, think of me as a man."

"I do," he said. "I must. You are a man."

I tried to laugh again, but it came out as a sort of *splut*, meaning nothing, except perhaps dismay. "I want that sexual kiss," I said. "And a lot more. What does that make me?"

"A pervert," he said levelly. "I love you." Without a pause, without a change of expression.

"What does that make you?"

He stuck there for a minute, still eye to eye. What I didn't know was what he was struggling with, or whether he was struggling at all. Surely it wasn't like Doron to look for excuses or try to make it easier for himself. But what made me think I knew what Doron was like? "It makes me a potential pervert," he said at last, "in a state of severe temptation."

"What makes the difference?"

"I resist it," he said. "You deliberately provoke it." I saw him swallow. I had gotten to him that much, at least.

Somehow when I wasn't noticing we had looked away from each other's eyes. "Even if I were willing," he said carefully, "to commit what I know to be a sin, it would be a very foolish thing for me to do. I don't know if you're familiar with the Selector's Code."

"No," I said. "I didn't notice that in the *Manual*." My throat was dry. *Selectors must be held to a higher standard.* I couldn't stop myself from adding (giving away more fear than I'd known I had), "It says Selectors aren't eligible for Selection."

"Just so. But a Selector is always liable to be degraded from office for actions unbecoming a Selector. After that—" His eyes came back to mine with a completely different look—like a child, not daring to plead for pardon. "After that, I could be selected for Punishment, though not for Bliss; and I'd be almost certain to be selected. Quite certain, I think I can say." He clasped his hands loosely on his ankles. "It's not in the *Manual*; that's why you didn't see it."

"Who—ah, who would—report you? Is that the word?"

His smile flickered. " 'Denounce' is the word. There would be plenty of volunteers. Selectors are not highly popular."

"Nobody would have to know," I heard myself say quietly.

He looked at me again, that naked look. "Is it worth the risk?" It was a question; he was asking, not dismissing. "The risk would be all mine," he added. Not complaining, just clarifying. Visitors were not eligible for Selection.

He was asking me if I would risk condemning him to decades of uninterrupted torture so I could have the pleasure of an affair with him—an affair that I would drag him into against his judgment and his principles. I tried not to feel resentful at the implication. He knew me no better than I knew him. How could he be sure that I wouldn't be willing to do it? How could I be sure? "Come with me," I said. "We can take the next starship out of here."

I had thought his face was already expressionless, but suddenly something was wiped out of it, leaving it still more bare. Honest as a skull. "God," he said, "is as much God on a starship as on Bimran."

"You mean Doron is as much Doron."

"I mean a sin is as much a sin," he said doggedly.

So there we were. Perfect freedom. "And to you I'm a pervert," I said, getting it straight. "A would-be-fornicating pervert. You're a Selector. If I were a Bimranite, would you—"

"Don't." He put his hand on mine, briefly but very positively. After a moment he said, "I'd give you a fair chance. We don't entrap people. We do allow for change. Signs of genuine change will always postpone Selection."

"But if I were—ah, incorrigible, you'd—"

"Yes, I would." He wouldn't let me say it, but he could say

it himself. "Of course I would." For that one sentence, his voice throbbed and shook with bitterness and his face burned. Then it was a skull again, a beautiful, brown-toned, bearded skull. His eyes ran over me, not too slow, not too fast.

"At least you don't believe in hell," I said. "We can both be grateful for that." At the moment I could imagine nothing more hideous than Doron trying to convert me.

"Yes," he said, still looking at me.

"Does it bother you a lot—my being a terrible sinner?"

He had clasped his slim hands again, and now he looked down at them. He was silent for what seemed a long time. "It's very complicated," he said; "the way I feel."

"You're very young," I said on impulse. Suddenly it mattered that I had been born a millennium before him. He was very young, and dying fast. They were all so ephemeral, these planetbound. How could they learn anything?

He raised his eyes. "Do you think it's likely to get any simpler?"

"No," I said.

≈ 17 ≈

When the techniques have been perfected, there is every reason to anticipate that Selection can be applied to all Bimranites (even, with suitable modifications of procedure, to Selectors). Until that time, we are limited to the Selection of the clearest cases. This, of course, applies both to Bliss and to Punishment. However, it must be recognized that sin is inherently easier to identify than virtue. The probability is that Selection for Punishment will be extended more rapidly than Selection for Bliss.

—*From* Revised Manual for Selectors,
Working Draft, Conclusions.

I didn't go to my own quarters after I said good-bye to Doron. I didn't want to face my own thoughts alone yet. I headed for Leona's door instead, and met the landlord coming out of it. "Nice day, Korlo," I said.

"Nice day," he answered, with his diffident smile. I thought he looked worried.

Leona certainly did. "Come on in, Liss. Sit a minute."

"What's the trouble?" That's one way to put off your own trouble, look at somebody else's.

She chuckled hoarsely. "Shows, does it? Well, it's not trouble, it's puzzlement. I've told you about Korlo's cousin at the Selection Center."

"Right." I sank uneasily onto a mushroom.

She settled herself on the other and tapped her fingers on her thighs. "Well, he heard my name mentioned."

"Who mentioned it? What did they say?"

"Couple of Selectors talking about what they call the problem of idolatry." She blew out her lips in a puff of breath. "To be precise, one of them said—I'm quoting this third-hand, you understand— 'If we want to get rid of idolatry in Bimran City, we should get rid of Leona Porlock.' "

"Slud! Is that as toxic as it sounds?"

She laughed. "No, it's not, thank Athena. They're not going to Select me, if that's what you're thinking. And I never heard of Selectors assassinating anybody; not their style. But there are a couple of things it *could* mean that I don't much like." She paused. "You know, I think I'd feel better if they'd said 'that fat old starshipper.' 'Leona Porlock' sounds too much like formal recognition."

"So what could they do to you?"

"They could refuse to renew my visitor's permit. That would get rid of me fast enough. It's only thirteen days from expiration." She made inarticulate grumbling noises. "Blast that bureaucrat that wouldn't renew it for me early! And the other thing they can do is scare everybody away from me." She shook her head slowly side to side, rejecting a piece of the reality she'd fallen into. "They've already scared Korlo. He came to tell me as a friend—and to apologize for how unfriendly he's going to be from now on."

"Slud, Leona! Does he want you to move out?"

"He's not going to evict me—not yet, anyway. He just doesn't think he can afford any more friendly chats." She looked at me darkly from under her bangs. "Now, don't *you* get judgmental, Liss. It was a brave thing for him to come and warn me. He could have just started cold-shouldering me and I'd never have known why." She went back to shaking her head—like sweeping a handwriter backward across a sheet of paper; trying to erase the past.

I watched her unhappily. I didn't like seeing Leona this way, and I didn't like the implications of what she was telling me—that Bimranite friendship wasn't something for a starshipper to rely on; that *not eligible for Selection* didn't mean *safe*.

"Well." She slapped her legs decisively. "The first thing I've got to do is get that permit renewed—or find out I can't. I'll know where I stand then. And if they do renew it, I'll have my options open. The next thing is, I'll do a little hanging around the spaceport. You know there's another starship docked. The *Pilgrim*."

"Oh, hey—" I stopped myself. What right did I have to say *Don't go?* I'd just been inviting Doron to leave Bimran with me, and I certainly hadn't thought of asking Leona's permission.

She gave me a quizzical look. "But I wouldn't be doing Korlo any kindness if I trotted off to the spaceport five minutes after he visited me. I can wait a few days." She smiled grimly. "Cheer up, girl. The worst that can happen is it's the end of another world for me. Nothing serious."

Sarelli wasn't where I expected to find him in the Park for our next lesson, but Shray was. She came bustling across the moss very purposefully. I stood my ground and met her with a frosty "Nice day."

"Oh, I'm so glad to find you, Liss! You're not too busy?"

"Apparently not."

Her bland little face squinched itself into a pucker of trouble. "I hesitate to mention this to you—"

She did hesitate, looking to me for help with such a lost expression that I melted a little. "Go on. What's wrong?"

"Well, it isn't *wrong*, of course, everything works together for good, but I can't help feeling concerned. It's—perhaps you heard?—"

"No, I haven't heard."

"Yes, I see. Well, it's—" She lost her voice, swallowed hugely, and got past the lump at the second try. "It's Morit." Her face collapsed into a pool of desolation. "He's been taken to the Selection Center."

My stomach lurched. "How do you mean, 'taken'?"

"We were dining in that open-air restaurant on the east side of the Park, you know?—yesterday evening, quite early, it was so beautiful yesterday—and a Selector came up to us and asked Morit to go with her to the Selection Center."

"And he went? Just like that?"

Her hands clutched each other, groping for consolation. "Yes, yes, of course. What else would he do? And he hasn't come back." She looked bewildered, as if gravity had suddenly turned her loose. "Morit has so many friends, of course. We'd, we'd know if he had come home."

"Doesn't he get a trial or something? A hearing?"

Her face reconstructed itself. "We don't know," she said brightly, "why they invited him, of course. Morit is such a *good* man. And we know that reality is what we make it. He's been under consideration as a candidate, we found that out recently."

"A candidate?" I said blankly.

"A candidate for Selection." She wavered and tensed herself. "I mention this to you, Liss, because you have a different position. As an offworlder, I mean. And you've been so kind and interested." I felt my hackles begin to rise. Instinct of self-preservation. "And I believe—I have the understanding that—that you have contacts, you're acquainted—you know a Selector. You could ask what's, what's—" Her face crumpled again.

I didn't like her any better than I had before. But she was hurting, and there was too much hurting going on already. I reached to put my arms around her in a hug that couldn't console but might at least comfort.

And she shied away from me, horror-struck.

I dropped my hands. "Don't worry, I'm not going to rape you."

"Oh, I, I didn't think that! It just—"

"Wouldn't look right, would it?" I finished for her. "I'll see what I can find out, Shray. How can I reach you?"

"Just leave a note at the message office over there—next to the fruit shop where we met, you remember? I stop by there often." Her eyes were filling up with tears. "I must go, I won't keep you, I—" She struggled for a smile. "Thank you, Liss."

I found that I didn't know how to reach Doron. I wasn't going back to the Selection Center unless my own life depended on it, and probably not then. I tried sending him a message, and was told that message offices didn't deliver to the Selection Center. Which was interesting. And even if I'd seen Sarelli—and I didn't see him—I wouldn't have asked his advice on this one. I had the powerful feeling that the fewer Bimranites knew about Morit's problem, the fewer people would get hurt.

Besides, I felt just as powerfully that if I wanted to see Doron—and I did!—I'd see him. I'd look up from whatever I was doing and there he'd be. Any minute now.

So I wasn't surprised when I saw him far down the street and coming my way. Not exactly how I'd pictured it, but close enough. I didn't run to meet him or even wave. We came together slow and easy, particles sliding along our tracks.

"It's not a nice day," I said, before he could speak. Part of his smile lingered, just at the corners of his eyes—he could still greet me with a smile, he was still somehow glad to see me—but the rest of his face was instantly ready for trouble.

"Can I help you?"

"Yes. You can tell me what's happened to Morit."

It wasn't what he'd expected. He was so transparently surprised that I was suddenly almost floating, relieved of a weight I hadn't known I was carrying. "Let's talk," I said, and led the way to a bench under a little rain shelter, one of those handy Bimran places where you could have privacy in public. "Yesterday evening," I said, "a Selector took Morit to the Selection Center. *Asked* him to go, and he went."

"How did you hear about it?"

"Shray was with him. She told me this morning. I—" I was about to say, *I promised to find out what happened to him,* but I didn't. "I don't understand," I said. How many times had I said that on Bimran? "You said you only Select extreme cases. Morit is a nobody. He hasn't done enough bad or good or anything else to show on the graph."

"I should have said, 'extremely clear cases.' " He looked troubled, and well he should. "Perhaps I haven't explained things well enough. Perhaps you haven't read the relevant parts of the *Manual.* Selection is based on an individual's actions."

"I understand *that.*"

"Do you? On the actions themselves—not on what went before or came afterward. Not on motives or intentions, and not on consequences."

"I see that, but—" I stopped. But had I seen it before the middle of my sentence? Actions in a vacuum. If there's a commandment against dropping stones off bridges and you drop a stone, it doesn't matter whether it hits somebody's head or not; you've broken the commandment. Extremely clearly. "Those people on the table," I said. "You talked about the things they'd done, the damage they'd caused, the lives they'd messed up. You made me think they were really nasty people who did really nasty things. And Sarelli told me they were mostly from Northtown. I thought, all right—predators, parasites, child-abusers. Now it turns out your idea of a horrible criminal is silly little Morit. Are they all a bunch of Morits out there on that table?"

"It's not like that, Liss." I saw his hand move as if he were about to make a gesture, and still itself again. "You probably realize," he said, "that Morit's was the case I was assigned to and then withdrawn from. And no, Morit is not my idea of a horrible criminal. But please understand one thing before we go any further—" (I choked a little gasp of a laugh. Going further, were we? On our way to where?) "We don't know," he said, "I don't know, what Morit's present status is. I had no idea he'd been brought in. It's quite possible, probable in fact, that he's merely being questioned. That happens sometimes. I told you his case has been absorbed into a larger investigation. I'm not part of that investigation, but I know it involves a considerable number of individuals, and I know it's focused on a single sin."

"What sin?"

"Idolatry. Morit may be a silly little person, as you call him—I rather think he is—but that doesn't exempt him from the necessity of keeping the Commandments. And whether or not he's kept them himself—and remember, we don't know yet—his information will be useful for the investigation."

"No coercion," I said. "I read that much of the *Manual*. There's supposed to be no coercion in gathering information."

"That's exactly right."

"So why was he hauled off to the Selection Center? That looks coercive to me."

"But he wasn't hauled off. You told me yourself, Liss, by Shray's account he was *asked* to go. That's standard procedure. Of course—" he hesitated— "it's conceivable that he has been Selected. For Punishment or for Bliss." He stood up. "I'll find out his status and let you know. I can do that much."

"Wait," I said. But it came out almost as a whisper, and he was already gone, a slim straight figure moving down the street without a backward glance. I'd meant to ask him what this idolatry nonsense actually meant. Worshipping pseudo-gods, Sarelli had said. Did that include Morit's vague wimp of a God and Shray's mushy Oneness? Did *worship* include whatever it was that Vailid's audience did around their blue table? Was Corriogaskula an idol?

I looked for Leona and didn't find her. It felt strange, standing on her entrance mat and rapping the knuckles of my fist against her door with no response. At Bimran doors there was no way for a visitor to call up an entry message, no way to know if there was somebody inside waiting for you to go away. Korlo wasn't visible, either. I wandered toward the message office by the fruit shop, keeping a few streets away from the Park because I wasn't in the mood to encounter Sarelli. I could at least let Shray know that I'd made inquiries. But as I started into the message office, Shray popped out of it.

"Oh, Liss—Nice day!—did you have a message for me? I was just going to send you one, and I saw you coming. Isn't it marvellous?"

I always had the feeling that Shray and I were talking

about different things. "What's marvellous?" She didn't look as if anything marvellous had happened to her recently. She was twisted as tight as she'd been this morning.

"Oh, I thought you would know, I thought you were coming to tell me. Morit is home again." She produced a brittle laugh. "Isn't it chilly this afternoon? I haven't seen him myself, but a neighbor saw him come home in a float-car."

I made some sort of inane noise. "Yes, well, I was told they probably just wanted to question him."

She gave me a sharp look. "Question him? What does that mean?"

"I don't know," I said. "I'm just a visitor here. At least it means they didn't Select him."

She shivered, one quick spasm. "You, ah, you haven't heard anything else?" She was staring at me with anguish-brightened eyes.

I sucked my lower lip. The dumbest thing you can do is get involved in local troubles, every starshipper knows that. But she needed to know. "There's a major investigation going on," I said. "It's focused on idolatry. They're looking at a lot of people."

A noise like the broken half of a sob came out of her. Then she pulled herself together with a little shake. "Well, of course," she said primly, "Morit would want to give all the help he could."

We come here to see our future, Sarelli had said. I wondered if Morit had been a regular visitor to the Selection Center. Probably not; he wouldn't want to face that brutal a reality. But as soon as I formulated the thought I found myself shaking my head like a Bimranite, telling myself, *No, that's wrong.* Of course Morit would visit the Selection Center; it was the proper thing to do. His way of not facing it was inventing a God who wouldn't allow anybody to suffer, with the possible exception of masochists. You had to give Morit credit. It must take a lot of serious mental gymnastics to look at those people on the table and say, "They're not really suffering." I wondered if he could still say that today.

But if I were a Bimranite, would I have done any better? Living with that fear day after day, year after year. And it doesn't take any acrobatics of the mind to conclude that other people aren't really in pain. In fact, it takes a lot of mental effort and education, starting at about age one, to learn that other beings are capable of pain at all. A lot of people are never really convinced. All Morit had done was apply the principle backwards and decide that God wouldn't allow *him* to feel pain either. But that's an idea very easy to disprove.

I didn't doubt that by this time Morit had made his deal. Signs of genuine change, according to the *Manual,* were always enough to postpone Selection. It was Morit's friends who had the urgent worries now, provided they were close enough to reality to notice. No big surprise that he hadn't wanted to face Shray, after the information he must have given at the Center.

"Rainbow Man!" somebody called. "Are you going to the concert, Rainbow Man?"

It was dusk when I came out of the concert hall—that wonderful, strange time when you find yourself briefly on the very limb of a rotating planet, between light and dark. I was glad I'd gone in. I felt better now, washed by the music, ready for the sounds of the world outside. There was laughter, calls between friends, a mellow snore of distant thunder. Someone stepped into my path, and it was Doron.

"There's something I need to tell you," he said. "Now."

"I already heard that Morit's been released."

He didn't seem to notice what I'd said. Bimranites milled around us, the concert crowd separating into little groups, chattering their opinions of the afternoon and their plans for the evening. "Over here?" Doron suggested, and we eased our way through the cheerful voices and sat down on a hard Bimran bench on a patch of tough Bimran moss a little back from the pavement.

We looked at each other. "I told you," Doron said, "that offworlders can't be Selected."

It's interesting; a few spoken words really can drop your body temperature significantly. "Yes, you told me that. Were you wrong?"

"I was wrong, Liss." I saw his teeth set tight for an instant. "There's one situation—" He broke off. It was the first time I'd ever heard Doron fail to finish a sentence.

I stood up. If I'd been standing up, I'd have sat down. "Don't apologize. Just tell me what the hell you didn't tell me."

He was standing up too by the time I finished. "If a visitor is clearly and materially contributing to the sins of Bimranites, that visitor should be urged to leave Bimran as soon as possible. Any visitor who refuses such urging should be considered, for purposes of Selection, a native Bimranite." He kept a steady eye contact. He was reciting from the *Manual*, of course. I should have scanned it more carefully. And that was it. He had nothing to add.

"Am I contributing to the sins of Bimranites?" My voice was a little thick. "What is it—clearly and—"

"Materially," Doron said. "Yes, you are."

I wasn't cold now, I was hot. "How?"

"You manufacture idols," he said levelly, as if it were a

statement that meant something. "And you—it could be argued—"

"Wait a minute," I said. "What's this 'manufacturing idols' stuff?"

"The things you weave," he said. "They're used by a group of idolators in Bimran City. And there's evidence that the practice is spreading."

"That's silly, Doron. They don't worship those little toys. They use them as aids in meditation, or something like that."

He shook his head. "It may sound silly if you don't understand idol-worship. A physical idol is always a representation or a channel, not an object of worship in itself. No one ever prayed to a statue; they prayed *through* the statue. That's exactly what these idolators do with your gold weaves, whether they call it meditation or anything else."

"All right, what does that have to do with me? I don't tell people how to use them. I don't *know* how they use them. I just make the things."

"In itself," he said, "it wouldn't be enough. But it could be argued that you encourage fornication."

"Oh, it could, could it? Do you argue that way?"

"That doesn't matter," he said. "It could be so argued. Liss, don't be angry. Or do be angry; but listen. Do you understand what I'm telling you?"

"Yes. No. Are you urging me to leave Bimran?"

"Yes."

We stared at each other, as if we were both surprised. "You mean if I don't get out, you'll send me to your torture chamber?" I was trembling all over. At the moment there didn't seem to be any difference between fear and anger.

"Liss," he said, "there's one thing more. It could be argued—"

"It could be argued! Don't you have the guts to make a straight statement?"

He closed his lips tight for a moment, and I saw that he was trembling too, a barely perceptible shiver like a stressed filament in the loom. Then he said in the same equable voice, "It could be argued that you have corrupted a Selector."

Nobody made straighter statements than Doron. "Do you think I've corrupted you?" I asked him.

"No." And maybe no one but I would have noticed the quiver in his voice.

All right, then. Blood pressure, heartbeat, stop the adrenalin. Doron was probably using all those techniques already, and there was *still* a quiver. "You're telling me," I said carefully, "that we're both in trouble." Selectors were held to higher standards than other people. I wondered if Doron would be called on to prove his purity by selecting me for Punishment.

And there were no laws on Bimran. That knowledge ran through me like a drink of supercooled liquor. I had never thought through the implications. There were no laws on Bimran—and it wasn't just the slums of Northtown that were left to their own devices. Visitors had no legal safeguards—not against Selection, not against anything else—only custom and luck and the Selectors' own regulations.

"I think you were right," Doron said constrictedly. "I *am* young. Very young or very stupid. It's not as if this were a new regulation. It's just that I never thought of its being applied in this way. I've never known it to be applied at all."

"Are they going to apply it? Have they applied it already?"

He moved his head a little, shaking off my impatience.

"It's a judgment, Liss, it's not automatic. I've told you, only a tiny fraction of the population are ever selected. But—"

"But—?"

"In a case like this—and especially now—"

"Why especially now?"

"There's considerable feeling against offworlders among some Selectors. It's known that the leader of the idolators is from Gantry Four and receives support from the Ishian planets. Liss—" His eyes pressed into me, gentle black holes in reverse. "There's a starship in docking orbit—"

"Shut up!" I squeezed my fists tight, to get a grip on myself. "I thought you weren't part of this investigation."

"I didn't know any of this until I started making inquiries about Morit today. One of my colleagues was kind enough to warn me. You were seen leaving a meeting of idolators, Liss."

I hooted an angry laugh. "I thought I was going to a concert! Who's this colleague—the man with the red beard?"

"Yes. He's a—very careful observer. Very thorough."

"And he was kind enough to warn you! You know what that sounds like, Doron? Like he wanted to know if you'd pass the warning on to me. And you did it, you turned straight around and did it. Five will get you twenty he's observing us right now."

"I had to warn you," Doron said. "The docked starship is called the *Pilgrim*. It may be leaving in a few days—"

"Come with me."

"I was trained for my job," he said. "I'll stay with it."

"You said you loved me."

"Forget that. Please forget that."

"Why?"

"You have to leave Bimran." Which might or might not be an answer to the question.

"I don't know," I said stonily. "I haven't done anything wrong. And you keep telling me Selectors are very careful not to make mistakes. Maybe it's time to prove that."

Leona must have been watching for me. I'd barely started pacing my floor when she was on my entrance mat. I let her in and she sank immediately into a mushroom. "The *Pilgrim*'s leaving tomorrow morning. I intend to be on it, Liss." Her voice was flat. "I advise you to be on it, too."

My mouth was dry. Everything Sarelli had taught me about salivation seemed far away and unimportant. "You really think it's that bad?"

"Worse. It's not just that they won't renew my visitor's permit; they've canceled it on the grounds that I'm a resident of Bimran. That means I'm eligible for Selection." She opened her mouth wide in a dry cackle. "Leona Porlock, the well-known idolator, now eligible for Selection. How do you like *that?*"

My mind answered with such a blank, I had to struggle to make a word out of it. "Why?"

She looked at me as if I'd just unhooked her mooring line. *At loose ends* has a serious meaning in space. "How do you mean, 'Why?'?"

"I thought they wanted to get rid of you, Leona. Why shouldn't they just let you go?" Visitors contributing to the sins of Bimranites should be urged to leave Bimran. But that was only a *should,* not a *must.*

"What good would that do them?" Her voice had turned harsh. "Give them a bit of a bad name in the cluster, maybe, but I doubt if they're even thinking about that. I've been contaminating Bimranites. You think they'd let me walk away unpunished? As far as the Selection System is concerned, I'm a big fat object lesson, just when they need one. Seems they're starting quite a crackdown on idolatry."

"I know." And if Migration Control conveniently decided to turn a visitor into a resident, there wouldn't be any chance of a good object lesson getting away.

"Fornication, too. *Trojan* Liss, Rainbow Man, well-known pervert. Nobody's better known than the Rainbow Man."

"Slud!" I said.

"Of course, they haven't canceled your visitor's permit yet. Or at least they haven't told you so. But——"

"But I haven't *done* anything, Leona! How can I be a pervert?"

She shrugged. "You've seen what's on the tables at the Selection Center, Liss. Object lessons. After the *Pilgrim,* there may not be another starship for months—maybe years. You want to risk it?"

I stood silent. It probably didn't show to Leona, but I was pushing at a perfectly transparent, perfectly immovable wall. No, I didn't want to risk that. Forty, fifty years of agony, with not a nanosecond of relief. Hell was real; it was right down the river at the Selection Center. But if I was in trouble, Doron was in trouble.

Leona leaned toward me. "Liss, I've been here twelve years, and I've never been scared before. I'm scared. I'm scared for my fat old self, and I'm scared for you, girl." She slapped my knee. "I've talked to the *Pilgrim*'s head docker. They've got room for seventeen passengers, with a chance to buy in, and they'll take all comers. I've already booked my place. Come with me. Tonight."

I wet my lips, or tried to. "I'll wear my brown walking-suit," I said.

≈ 18 ≈

Selection must be based on consistent patterns of action. Signs of genuine change will always postpone Selection, but only long enough to determine whether a new pattern has truly been established.
—*From* Revised Manual for Selectors,
Working Draft, Chapter 3.

The brown walkingsuit wasn't the only precaution we took. It was Leona's idea that we should walk—"If you ask me, they monitor every floatcar to the space-port"—and do it shortly before dawn. "We'd be mighty obvious if we went now," she said. "Nobody goes to the spaceport after dark. Let's get some sleep first and take our walk when there's nobody on the streets."

"They don't have night patrols?" I asked. It was funny how quickly you could start thinking like a fugitive.

Leona snorted expressively. "This is Bimran, remember?"

"Yes, but, Leona—if we're a couple of major sinners, and they know the only starship docked is pulling out tomor-row—"

"But they don't. The *Pilgrim*'s not scheduled to leave for another week." She looked at my face and erupted in a belly laugh. "It pays to pay, didn't anybody ever teach you that? I've not only bought in, I made a little extra contribution to the *Pilgrim*'s operating expenses. Hermes isn't my god for nothing. There's been an unannounced schedule change. They don't have any sightseers out or major deals pending—thank Hermes!—so there's nothing to keep them." She patted my shoulder. "The Selection Corps is not used to handling starshippers, anyway. Get some sleep."

I didn't even try Sarelli's sleep techniques. I had a few pills left from the *Trojan*, and somehow that seemed more appropriate now. Mentally, I'd already abandoned Bimran. But with the pill in my mouth, I couldn't swallow. I spat it out and stood looking at it on the palm of my hand. There it was, that invisible wall I couldn't get through or around. If I was in trouble, Doron was in trouble.

I packed my gold—the few kilograms I had on hand—my off-Bimran currency, a few toiletries, and my footboard into the shoulder carry. And the *Manual*. I couldn't leave that behind. It wouldn't take them long to trace the proper owner. Corrupted Selector's own *Manual* found in fleeing pervert's quarters. Wouldn't look right, would it?

I kept changing my clothes. First the brown walkingsuit. I didn't want to see how I looked in it, but I felt obliged to check. Could I pass for a Bimranite in the dark? I activated my mirror and stifled a small burst of laughter. This wasn't supposed to be funny, and I wasn't supposed to be hysterical. But really, could that drab, awkward person be me?

All right, that was the idea. I hadn't pointed out to Leona—had almost forgotten it myself—that technically I wasn't a fugitive. I'd been officially urged by a Selector to leave Bimran. If there was any pretense of justice here—and there was certainly plenty of that—I should be allowed to leave openly. But I couldn't count on it. There were no laws on Bimran. What there were, were a bunch of Selectors out to purge the planet of offworlders. And I'd be abetting the

escape of Leona Porlock, the well-known Bimranite/
offworlder idolator. I stared at my own staring eyes. No, it
wasn't funny.

I deactivated the mirror and began to change my clothes.
There's always another option. If you can't get through the
wall, you can get along with it. Genuine change, the *Manual*
said. Signs of genuine change are always enough to postpone
Selection. Why shouldn't a butterfly undergo another metamorphosis? I could go straight to the Selection Center, find
Redbeard, and abjure my sins or whatever they were. I
could stop weaving sunlights and try to buy back the ones in
circulation. I'd be more than happy to break off anything
like friendly relations with Vailid's sympathizers, if any of
them survived the purge. I could do good works in Northtown. But I wasn't going to wear sackcloth and ashes. Doron
had assured me there was nothing wicked about bright
clothes. If I was going to say these things to Redbeard, and
mean them, I wasn't going to do it looking like a little brown
robot beetle.

Ticktick, tick, tickticktick. No, it wasn't somebody trying to
break in, it was one of those weird meteorological noises that
Bimran was full of. Falling precipitation can make a racket
when it hits. And it's really not strange that you can hear
wind; that's what a lot of sound is, after all—moving air. But
it still took me by surprise sometimes. Something sang a
resonant crescendo and dopplered away like the flying musicians in the Park, and I could hear the *tickticktickety* of
whatever it was hitting the outside walls again.

I activated the mirror and studied myself critically. No
doubt about it, the deep reds were good colors for me. I'd see
Leona safe on board the *Pilgrim,* and then I'd head for the
Selection Center, taking the first floatcar I could find. "Butterfly" was a metaphor, not a statement of fact. And surely

Selectors could have friends; I wouldn't have to stop seeing Doron altogether. This was one world I didn't have to throw away.

But it wasn't smart to be too aggressively colorful—and certainly not to wear anything that would make a Selector think of sex. Instead of the red and chocolate swirls, I'd do better in my low-key green and ivory coverall. The only trouble was, it wasn't water-repellent. If it was still raining when we started for the spaceport, I'd have to wear a guard-cape. I changed slowly, filling up time. *Tickety tickety*, Bimran kept saying outside.

When the watch in my ear finally chimed, both the weather and I had long since settled into stasis—so much so, I almost resented having it broken. I stood up stiffly, feeling heavy and disarticulated. *It's not hard to tranquilize yourself.* Sarelli had told me that, way back in our first lesson. *You can do it with a temporary lie.* I hadn't known what he meant then. A temporary lie was one you couldn't believe very long—one you knew you were going to retract. Doron was right, as I'd known he was; I had to leave Bimran. Once you've unfurled your wings from the chrysalis, the next metamorphosis is death. Death or worse. I picked up the brown walkingsuit and began to change.

There was no use advertising anything to the neighborhood. I deactivated the light before I unshuttered a viewport. It was brighter outside than I'd expected. The clouds must have broken after the storm. I could see that Leona's door was still shut. And then I realized why everything in the courtyard glistened whitely. It wasn't wetness; it was ice.

I met Leona at her door. It was too dark to read her face. "How slick is it?" she asked softly.

"Slick. Do you want to wait till morning and take a float-car?" There was a strange ordinariness about everything, the way we spoke and moved, the way I felt. *This is how people die,* I thought. *Nothing special.*

"Come in, a minute." Her hand closed on my wrist and pulled me into the darkness of her room. "Here." There was distaste in her voice. "You might as well carry it. I doubt if I could look convincing."

I took what she handed me. It seemed to be nothing but a modeled handgrip with a short snout like a drinking tube at one end, but heavy as solid gold. "What am I supposed to do with it?"

"If we get in a really tight spot, point it at somebody and look threatening. It's a shover."

I turned it in my hand, feeling it out. "What does it do?"

"Shoves people around. No, don't laugh. The toxic thing can be deadly. It pressurizes an air column. No good in a vacuum, but in this atmosphere it can whomp you with about ten kilonewtons. Thank Athena, it's got a very short range."

"Where the slud did you get this, Leona? *Why* did you get this, Leona?"

I heard her snort. "You sound like a pious Bimranite, girl! I decided a long time ago that on a world with no laws and no police, you'd better be prepared to defend yourself if necessary. Now, I may have been wrong; I've never had occasion to use it. And I don't think we're going to run into any trouble. But just in case anybody tries to stop us—"

"If they try to stop us," I said, "they'll probably have bigger guns than this. Where *did* you get it?"

"Don't embarrass me. You know offworlders can do things respectable Bimranites wouldn't dare. I don't think there are very many of these little toys circulating outside the Selection Corps, but—"

"Selectors go around with these?"

Leona chuckled. "Your ears prick up every time some-body says 'Selector.' You mean, does Doron have one of these in his pocket when he's giving you those soulful looks? I don't know. But Selectors certainly have the best hardware on the planet. Tools of the trade. As far as I can tell, there's just a very small trickle of it that gets into the black market. I mean, what would be a black market on a normal planet. Now: are you willing to use that thing if the need arises?"

"Show me how."

"Here and here—feel the dents? Press them both at the same time to ready. After that, all it takes is a squeeze. Press either dent again to safety it. Ready to go?"

"You don't want to wait and take a car?"

She hesitated. "Let me try it."

I led the way out and stood aside for her. She took a tentative baby step. On the second one, her foot slipped and she lurched against me, grabbing blindly for a hold. We staggered into the wall, both gasping our expletives, not to shout them. But we didn't fall. Leona adjusted her center of gravity with care. I heard her breathing hard. "My fault," she said. "I can do better than that. Let's go."

Feeling our way step by step, we made it down the length of the courtyard and turned into the glistening street. "This happens every year or two," Leona said, laboriously conver-sational. "Ice storm. You can get used to walking on streets coated with ice."

I laughed in protest. Ice was something created in refriger-ator units, or pointed out in mountain-sized blocks by tourist guides. Ridiculous for it to be smeared over a thoroughfare. My foot slid, and I clutched at Leona's arm.

She grunted. "Try to step where it crunches, not where it glides. Anything that looks rough is good. Hang on to me and go slow. I don't intend to fall." The hard metal in her voice surprised me. She laughed with a perceptible effort. "You'd think I had enough padding not to worry, wouldn't you? Trouble is, the same stuff makes it hard getting up again once I'm down. And the old bones could crack pretty easy. I wasn't born for this gravity."

"Oops!" I said, and giggled helplessly. "Sorry, I'm trying. I thought *I'd* be a help to *you.*"

"Slud!" She jerked at my arm, righted herself, and chuckled. "Toxic ice!"

We toddled hysterically, almost retching with laughter in the bursts of hilarity that punctuated our silence. Frantic with urgency, one baby step after another, zigzag and sidling down the street. *Reality is like this,* I thought. *Life and death, love and the nature of the cosmos, it all comes down to this: can we or can't we walk a hundred meters of icy street without falling?*

Leona was muttering through clenched teeth. "What?" I asked anxiously.

"Athena, protect us," she said aloud. "Hermes, give us good journey. Rab, help us make something out of this crap."

Once we reached the main street that led to the south bridge, the going was easy. A broad ice-free strip stretched down the middle of the street, a corridor of blackness in the starlit glimmer. "Thermostatic pavement," Leona said. She sighed hugely.

I echoed her sigh, and we both laughed. "I was beginning to think we wouldn't make it before daylight," I said. "Let's move."

Leona was able to keep up a brisker pace than I'd expected. Fifteen, twenty minutes and we'd be safe. I tried to concentrate on that, and on feeling warmer, helped by the warmth of the pavement and the vigorous walking. But now that there was no ice to keep my eyes on our feet and my mind on our balance, I was noticing how much we resembled the beginners' practice targets in some Ishi Three shooting gallery. The unlighted street was like a motionless, silent river, and we clattered down it like slow-moving beacons, transmitting *Here we are, here we are* to the world around us. Trapped on that strip of ice-free pavement (and a couple of meters didn't seem nearly as wide now as it had at first), we couldn't even take serious evasive action.

Left and right of us, ice glinted on the dim hulks of buildings, on crouched figures that turned out to be benches and recyclers and bushes, and tall figures that turned out to be post-trees with their leaves folded in for winter. Ahead, our orbit was laid out for us, the black channel of pavement, inevitable as gravity, swinging us slowly toward the bridge and the spaceport.

On the bare Bimran street, in the still Bimran night, even my softsoles made a noise, and Leona's shoes raised a racket that came back amplified from the building fronts. I could hear the river, too, a tremorous mumble that would never have carried this far by day. It was silly to pretend we could keep quiet, but somehow both of us were speaking in whispers now, when we spoke at all.

"Leona, if *we* can do this, why can't anybody, anytime?"

"Bimranites? Mostly because they think they can't. No, mostly because they don't want to. They grow up with the idea that somebody's watching them all the time; it doesn't occur to them they could do something and not be spotted. Besides, most people are happy here. Anybody who's thinking about leaving is probably already under surveillance." Suddenly she laughed, an almost-silent rasp of sound. "You know something? If I'd had any sense I'd have seen what was happening when they wouldn't renew my permit early.

Could have gotten out easy then. By now they've probably got automatic surveillance on me."

I went cold and hot—first scared, then angry. Were they playing with us? "Then why haven't they picked us up?"

She chuckled hoarsely. "Rab is looking out for us. You know one thing these ice storms do? They always mess up communications for hours. Change the surface characteristics of everything—emission, reflection, permeability, elasticity, you name it. Identification, transmission, reception go all to hell, if you'll pardon the expression. Surveillance systems won't be working very well right now."

"Thank Rab," I whispered. That was only partly sardonic.

The voice of the River Bimran grew louder, covering our whispers, damping the resonance of our footsteps. A little of the tension trickled out of me; we weren't quite so naked with that sound to snuggle into. But Leona was slowing. I thought it was tiredness from the fast walk, until her fingers clenched around my arm.

The bridge lay just before us—two luminous stripes separated by a span of nothing. On each side of the bridge the river glittered; ice-glazed rock and spurting spray caught every wandering photon and flung them back in flecks of light. Beyond, the ghostly faint glow of the spaceport's entry pylons stood like a gate to the promised land. But except for the pale luminous guidelines, the bridge itself was only an absence of light. Looking at that bridge, I had the feeling that if I stepped onto it I would cease to exist.

It took me a moment to notice that something was going on at the far end of it. A dim bulk smaller than a building and larger than a recycler, with movement around it—in the dark, at thirty meters or so, I couldn't make out more than that. Leona was tugging me persistently sideways, off the bare pavement and across the ice. This time neither of us laughed as we struggled to keep our balance.

There was a burst of light, and the scene at the end of the bridge lay in a pool of illumination. Half a dozen people stood and moved around a floatcar—one in black, another with a massive dark beard. I stood frozen to the spot, as if the ice storm had locked me there. "Down the bank!" Leona's harsh voice urged me. We scrambled across an icy stretch of paving or ground to that crucial elbow of this moment's world where the bank fell away to the river and the blank bridge sprang out across it. I clambered a few chancy steps down the bank, into the wild song of the river. "Help me," Leona panted.

My groping hand found what felt like support struts under the edge of the bridge, ice-covered and freezing cold. I locked my arm around one of them and reached my other hand to help Leona, bracing and easing her, step by step, down the bank. "What are we doing?" I asked.

"There's some kind of walkway under here for maintenance crews. Don't let go of me yet! All right, now I'm stable. Reach to your right."

"Is this it? Wait a second." I changed my grip to another strut, my sleeve ripping away from the ice of the first one with a sound I could hear even through the river's song. "Now feel this, Leona." I heaved her closer—we were really under the bridge now—and guided her hand.

"That's the handrail, I think." We had to almost bump heads to hear each other talk. The underside of the bridge was like an echo chamber, resounding with the river's cries. "You got a good enough grip to feel with your foot?" Leona asked.

I hung myself slantwise over a sloping strut, reached into

nothing with my right foot, and felt my left slip out from under me. I dangled, clutching at struts, too busy to make a noise, until my right foot found purchase on something level and solid. "Hey! I think I've got it!"

"Hurry up," Leona said grimly. "I'm about to slip."

I got both feet onto the solid surface and contorted myself off and under the strut I'd been hanging over, managing to keep a grip on it with both hands until I'd got my rear between my feet and could let go without flopping backward onto the icy rocks of the river. I couldn't have done that little maneuver my first week on Bimran; gravity does toughen you up. The surface was broad and gloriously ice-free. I rolled onto my front and reached for Leona.

Getting her on was a struggle for both of us. We sat side by side to recuperate. "Does this thing go all the way across?" I asked, when I got my breath.

"It'd better."

"What do we do at the other end?"

"Find out when we get there, won't we? But we better be getting. It's lightening up already. As long as they've got that flare lit, they won't be able to see much outside of it, that's the good part. Here, you stand up first and give me a hand."

I did. "Leona, did you see what I saw when that light went on?"

"A couple of Migration Controllers, a Selector, and at least three people getting pulled out of a floatcar. Not that you can tell Migration Controllers by looking, but I'd lay money on it."

"And I'd lay money that the one with the beard was Vailid. Unless she's got a clone brother on this planet. Close up, I probably wouldn't have recognized her."

Leona had struggled to her feet, almost pulling my arm out of the socket in the process, her grunts and grumbles lost

in the sound of the river. "And I doubt I'd recognize anybody at that distance," she said skeptically.

"Oh, yes, you would, Leona, you do it all the time. The
way she stood, the way she moved. Not at first—she was
disguised, and it wasn't just the beard. But then she straightened herself up and moved her arm, and it was Vailid."

"She's got her problems," Leona said, "and we have ours.
Thank Athena for this handrail."

I did mentally thank whoever had put it there. What we
stood on was a narrow catwalk, with the waist-high railing
on one side only. I felt my way along it slowly, Leona bump-
ing into me from behind. "Be careful," I shouted through
the river's resonant booming. "There's ice in spots."

"Noticed that myself! Nothing thermostatic here, it's just
the bridge protected it from the ice storm."

We shuffled the rest of the way without words, except for
my occasional cries of "Ice!" or "Duck your head—cross
strut!" The walkway thrummed with the river and our own
steps. In places—the iciest places—river spray showered us.
The bridge was just above our heads. A fan of radiance
showed where the light still shone at the end of the bridge,
and as we passed into and under it we could feel, more than
hear, steps and voices above us.

The bank beyond was blessedly unlit, with just enough
scattered light to help our slow, painstaking scramble off the
catwalk and up the icy roughness. This bank was steeper
than the other. We didn't even try to stay on our feet; we
crawled. Leona went first, with me pushing from below.
There was nothing frantic about our movements; there was
too much at stake to panic.

At the top we lay flat for a minute—or as flat as Leona
could get—watching the scene in the light. Yes, that was
Vailid in the thick beard and heavy hair that had been

popular on Gantry Four when I was there. She stood serene and commanding, one hand floating motionless as if it lay against an invisible screen a few centimeters from the float-car's side. The black-clad Selector and three officious-mannered individuals (obviously the Migration Controllers that Leona had spotted) looked petty beside her. There were more people now—the floatcar must have emptied out—five altogether of what were presumably Vailid's followers, nervously stirring. One of them was Shray.

I couldn't look away from her face. Her eyes went back and forth, Vailid to the Selector, Vailid to the Controllers, always back to Vailid. She had the look of a child whose parents have led her into the airlock without a suit and are now busy opening the outside hatch. Vailid was making a deal.

Leona's bulk stirred beside me. She forced herself up onto her knees. I got up cautiously—there wasn't much chance of their seeing us, they in their circle of light and we in the dark, but we had to be careful of sudden noises—and helped her to her feet. We locked arms and began our slow march.

The crunch of our feet on the ice was lost in the river noises. We kept along the bank, skirting the spaceport. This was Bimran; there were no fences or protective screens to keep out intruders. Docked ships were responsible for their own security, though the warehouses were said to have alarm systems. The scene on the end of the bridge shrank to a distant pool of brightness, half obscured by the entrance pylons. To our right was a nearer glow, and a dark shape above it—the *Pilgrim* lander, with its entry hatch open and a light that said *Welcome home*. We turned and hurried toward it.

We didn't speak. Frozen moss and stems crunched under our feet like shattering munchcakes, and then we were on the bare dry pavement of the spaceport, which, like any good spaceport pavement, slurped away all moisture before it could freeze. We broke into a trot. The light at the entry hatch looked unreal, something out of a children's game. We stepped into the warmth of the airlock, and two dockers with *"Pilgrim"* badges on their headbands raised their eyes from a board game that didn't look much different from the one we'd whiled away docking duty with on the *Trojan*.

"Took you long enough," one of them said to Leona. "Your friend want to sign on too?"

≈ 19 ≈

Selectors are authorized to use any degree of force that does not result in permanent impairment of the individual. Force should be applied only in extreme cases. At present, of course, most cases of Selection are extreme.

—*From* Revised Manual for Selectors,
Working Draft, Chapter 7.

L eona burst into a gasping cackle of relief.

"All right, let's get you checked in," the docker said impatiently. "All this data entry is supposed to be done before we lift."

"How long to liftoff?" I asked.

The other docker pointed at a pulsing orange display on the wall beside her: *Hours to liftoff: 1.697.*

I shrugged off my shoulder carry, set it at Leona's feet, and pulled my footboard out of it. "I'll be back," I said, and turned to the entry hatch.

Leona grabbed my arm. "What are you up to?"

"I'm going back for Doron." I looked at the dockers. "There's room for another, right?"

The verbal one spread his hands wide. "Anybody that gets here in time. That's up to seventeen, counting you two. But I'm telling you, if you don't get registered before lift, you may have to sleep in the corridor."

I stepped onto the footboard and slid out into the cold. Without Leona, I could make better time. I wasn't fragile; I could take a few tumbles if I had to. I pulled out Leona's gun, pressed the two dents, and pocketed it again. Ready for anything now.

Daylight was coming fast. I sped across pad and pavement and took my first tumble into the crusty riverbank vegetation. Too rough for a footboard here. I clipped it into my backsling—this walkingsuit had everything—and sprinted through the half-dark, retracing our path. Less than an hour point seven; I didn't have time to look for unknown shortcuts.

It was easier than I would have expected if I'd given myself the luxury of thinking about it. There was no light on the bridge now, and no movement visible either there or in the dim radiance of the ornamental pylons at the spaceport entrance. But I didn't want to be a silhouette for any possible observer. Several meters farther from the bridge than the spot where we had come up, I let myself slide down the bank until my head was below its top.

The trouble was, I kept sliding.

And now I did panic. The river howled below me. The bank was a nightmare chute studded with knobs that refused my clutching hands. Then my right foot wedged into a crevice and my right elbow found support on a stub of frozen plants. I clung flat and trembling, my tears slowly freezing my cheek to the icy rock it pressed against.

Leona had been more of a help to me than I'd realized—not just somebody to hang on to, but somebody not to panic in front of, somebody not to feel alone with. If I slid down this carnival-ride bank and hit the brutal river, there'd be nobody to know about it—not until they found whatever was left of me, smashed or frozen or drowned. Likelier and worse, half-drowned, half-frozen, half-smashed.

I'd thought I could edge myself along till I reached the bridge, but I'd been wrong. I needed better holds than I could find on this toxic cliff. But at least I wasn't sliding anymore. I began to grope upward with my left hand and foot, every movement cramped by the footboard on my back. Come on, Rab; I've made the mistake, now where's the profit?

Clutch and slip, clutch and slip, clutch, slip, and hold. It wasn't easy, it wasn't certain, but it wasn't impossible. A bud of calmness opened inside my chest, spreading its petals slowly. I worked my way up, sidling and up, until I heaved my head above ground level, nose to thorn with some prickly shrub at the bank's edge, and got my elbows solidly on the flat. Through the shrub's branches the sky was ghostly blue, the stars all gone. I took a deep breath.

Then it was a sidewise crawl along the edge of the bank, part of me on the level and part down the slope, until I hit the bridge and had to duck under to find the catwalk's struts. Then for a while I crouched on the catwalk, shaking with relief and cold, laughing in bursts through chattering teeth.

After that it was almost easy. Twice I heard or felt the low pulse of a floatcar on the bridge above me—the beginnings of the day's spaceport traffic. Bimranites got up early. But when I crawled up the bank on the city side and gingerly raised my head, both street and bridge were empty. I unslung my footboard and got moving, slapping debris and ice off my walkingsuit as I went.

The streets glittered. It was clear daylight. I felt dark in my drab brown—conspicuous by dullness. Doron would be at the Selection Center. I asserted that to myself as a fact, while another system of my brain worked on alternatives in case he wasn't.

Farther into the city, there were people, going about their business, doing their early morning things. It was comforting in a way, but I wasn't comforted. Brown isn't a color; it's the slush you get when you dump everything into the blender. Even drab, I thought people were looking at me. I was too disheveled for Bimran morning traffic. And I'd left my hair-sleeker in the shoulder carry. I sped on. If Doron wasn't in his private cubicle, I'd have to ask for him; I didn't have time to wander around the Center looking for him.

A man and a woman coming my way on the other side of the street were definitely interested in me. They had stopped their footboards maybe twenty meters off, talking earnestly and watching me approach. Now they snagged the next passerby. He turned to look my way, and they all consulted. I fell in behind a team of adolescent runners doing their morning trot, and followed them around a corner. Icy pavement, I was glad to find out, didn't affect the footboard. The runners slipped and laughed, but kept trotting. When the street forked I left them, took a few random turns, backed out of a dead end, and headed again toward Northtown and the Selection Center. The flat early sunlight made it easy to tell direction.

On these twisting streets there was only an occasional floatcar and a few people on foot. Most of the ones I met greeted me with reassuring Bimran cheerfulness. A stranger is a friend unless proved otherwise. *Unless proved otherwise, an individual is considered virtuous.*

I didn't know this neighborhood. I'd make better time cutting through the Park, with its wide-open spaces of level moss. I followed the streets that somehow looked Park-directed (What clues was I picking up on? I must have adapted to Bimran more than I knew) and in only a few minutes I came out into it. The moss was a sheet of granular gray-white, crisp and crackling under my footboard, so that I traveled with a continuous sound of little explosions. Action and adrenalin had warmed me. The air stung my face. Leona was right, it was a lovely climate. Off to my left, I could just see and hear the River Bimran, tossing arms of spray and singing to itself.

My footboard stopped so suddenly that I went headlong, ending up on my face in the ice. I had time to think—flying through the air and sliding across the snapping bristles of moss—that if the board had merely died it would have slid to a gentler halt; something had not just killed it but held it. So I was groping in the walkingsuit's unfamiliar pocket before I stopped sliding, and came up slipping and staggering but with Leona's little gun in my hand.

There were three of them, Redbeard in the middle, all in decent Selector black. Every one of them had something pointed in my direction. That was all I registered. While my consciousness was beginning to consider the practical and moral advisability of various courses of action and inaction, my hand was squeezing the gun grip spasmodically. One of the sidekicks jerked backward as if he'd activated a retrojet. Redbeard shouted something, drowned out by my mind's first coherent thought: *Selectors won't shoot to kill.* I zigzagged my weapon, squeezing again and again. All three had dropped to the icy moss—maybe to escape my shots, maybe because some of them had hit home. Sprays of shattered frost spouted around them, giving me the range. I aimed more consciously, stepping forward with every shot. I wanted my footboard; I didn't know how else I could get to the Selection Center and back to the spaceport in time.

There was a howl, and one of them jolted backward on

the ice and rolled into an awkward ball. Something thumped my arm, spinning me backward. I caught myself on the other arm, not going down completely, and rolled to my knees before I understood that my gun was gone and my right forearm flapping limply.

"Stay where you are," Redbeard rumbled. "I am asking you to come with me to the Selection Center."

That must have been straight out of the *Manual.* I crouched, looking for the gun. There it was, a good two meters to my right. He'd expect me to move that way, if I moved. But my footboard was just in front of me.

Redbeard was getting laboriously to his feet—I must have hit him somewhere—but the other two were still down. I snatched the edge of the footboard as I came up in a rush, and flipped it at him as hard as I could manage—not a good throw, but enough to put him off balance while I ran.

I was heading for the nearest edge of the Park, which was where the river disappeared for a stretch behind the apartments and skywalks of Riverside. Leona's voice replayed drummingly in my head: *Very short range. Very short range.* I wished I'd asked her what *very short* equaled in meters. The moss was crunchy under my pounding stride; as long as I hit hard, I didn't slip. I was counting on none of the trio being very fast on their feet just now.

My left leg shot out from under me, as if it had decided we were doing a kick dance, and I hopped, slid, skipped, but didn't fall. When I got my foot working again and pounded it down into the moss for a serious step, pain shot up my leg and I almost went down. But the leg didn't buckle. I kept on running.

I could hear nothing except the smash of my feet hitting frozen moss and ground, the gasp and hiss of my breath, and the wretched swishing of my walkingsuit, which made enough noise to cover the sounds of a whole squad of pursuers. Probably I'd done it all wrong. I should have gone for the gun. Or I should have tried to talk my way out of it, instead of shooting first. How was I to know? This wasn't the kind of thing I was good at.

At least I knew where I was, more or less. Deep in trouble, but close to Sarelli's apartment. And I had to stop. Every step I took meant stabbing myself again, straight up the leg and all the way now to the hip. Every breath insisted that it had to be the last at this speed.

People must be watching from at least some of those viewports in the buildings just ahead. Or refraining from watching. Farther down the Park I could see people, refraining from coming this way. Not three meters in front of me, somebody opened a door and promptly closed it again. *The hell with you,* I thought. I pelted past—stab step gasp, stab step gasp—and around the corner of the building. I came up against an ornamental pillar, not sure if I'd deliberately picked it to lean on or just shipwrecked on it, and hung there with my left arm around it and my head drooped to thigh level, getting back enough breath to straighten up and go on. Yes, I recognized this corner. And since nobody had come around it yet, the first thing was to get away from it. I began to jog.

I was feeling sick. All this time I had literally forgotten about my right arm, but the minute's rest had reminded me, with waves of ugly hurting that made the pain in my leg seem refreshingly straightforward. I turned down a narrow path and came to what I wanted: an intersection with a whole circle of pillars, radiating at least a dozen such paths. I trotted into the one that said *Sarelli* to me.

On these footpaths there were occasional people, the normal morning traffic of a residential section. I tried to look normal myself, Bimran normal: a solitary runner, disheveled from a brisk workout and maybe limping a little from a sore foot, but cheerful as always. A limp was acceptable; a broken arm was not. I concentrated on keeping it in a plausible position, and that helped keep my attention off the pain. People smiled at me, people said "Nice day," and I bobbed my head and grimaced in response.

If Redbeard and his crew were still after me, they must have lost the trail. There were no vehicle streets in this neighborhood, only the interlocking webs of footpaths. Overhead, translucent walkways crisscrossed between buildings, striping the paths below with wide bands of ocher and pale greens and blues. You could live in these places like a starship, never stepping outside, if that was what you wanted. My legs moved slower and slower, but I kept up a blundering run. What consciousness I could still control was so focused on the running that I almost passed Sarelli's building before the pattern of braided curves on its façade penetrated my neutral circuitry. Most distinct, most textured. I had to go back a few stumbling paces to the entrance. Nobody following me; nobody inside the lobby. I limped to Sarelli's door and planted my feet on his entrance mat.

When the door finally opened, I jerked backward before I recognized Sarelli. I'd never seen him dressed like this before—a loose home-robe of as dull a brown as my walkingsuit. Sarelli domestic; a different phenomenon from Sarelli public. "I need help, Sarelli," I said.

He didn't answer. After a moment he stepped back and I eased myself in, sliding the door shut behind me. I didn't want to look as scared as I surely did. If I'd taken more of his lessons, I'd be controlling my breathing and salivation better. The way Sarelli stood there, just balancing on his feet as if he felt the planet rolling underneath him—was that a learned skill too? I concentrated on slowing my heartbeat to a reasonable rate while I waited for him to say something.

But he didn't say anything. He turned and walked away from me, through another door that he closed behind him. A hot-cold feeling flowed downward inside me, a short, interior river. This was a bad time to be reminded of how alien I was here. It didn't much matter that we were genetically of the same species, that we shared a certain amount of common knowledge, a certain amount of common history, and something that could be described as a common language. It didn't even matter that we had danced together and laughed together under the stars. When it came time for real communication—which was probably something that happened to humans once a lifetime or so—what mattered was that we had learned to think and feel in different worlds.

There was a plump brown mushroom near the door I'd come in by, and I let myself down onto it. There are always decisions to make, according to Doron, and you always make them. I was deciding to trust Sarelli a little more than I distrusted him.

Quiet drummed inside my ears. I looked around vacantly. Three months on Bimran, and this was the first time I'd ever been inside a Bimranite home. First and last. Hard to get into, but it was a very open-feeling place on the inside, a wide room full of soft colors and space; nothing here of Sarelli's glitter and tightness. A silent beige floor, another mild brown mushroom—Bimranites didn't entertain many guests—a single viewport looking out onto the public footpath. And a ringing in my ears.

I pressed my good hand against the side of my head and took it away again. No, it wasn't just the tinnitus of silence drubbing at my eardrums. There was something going on—a liminal vibration that changed like distant voices. I turned my head, trying to get a fix on the direction.

Sarelli came back as lightly and steadily as he had gone, with a crumpled packet of something in his hands. He shook it out and tossed it down beside me. "Bubblesuit?" I asked. How could I be surprised? I hadn't been expecting anything.

"Yes." He was already kneeling. My breath caught when his hands went around my ankle. He tilted his face up to mine. "Bone's all right. Stressed, of course. What did you do to it? Torn ligaments and a split sinew. . . . Hurts, does it?"

"What am I supposed to do with the bubblesuit?"

He answered with something between a laugh and a whistle. His hands were still on my ankle, feeling it, shaping it. I'd always known his fingers would be extraordinary. "I can't heal this," he said. Teacher's voice. "You have to do it yourself."

"I know," I said. "I don't think I have that much time."

Now it was definitely a laugh. "I think you're right about that, Rainbow Man."

"There's the arm, too," I added. Make it sound light, Liss. No heavy stuff for Sarelli.

His hands closed on the arm I held out to him, feeling along it, probing with fingertips. My teeth had a good grip on the inside of my lip. Sarelli whistled, let go, and slid to his feet. "If you use that thing—" he flipped a finger at the bubblesuit— "pump it up tight. I suggest at least one-thirty-five kilopascals." He turned away.

I took a handful of the filmy thing, and my fingers clutched on it. "What am I supposed to *do* with this?" Never mind if I sounded frantic. Let him know.

"Do what you choose, Rainbow Man," he said over his shoulder. "Have you ever seen a rainbow?" He crossed the room with that balancing step and slid open a piece of the wall.

Now I knew what that faint, live vibrating had been. The music of the River Bimran poured in. Even from my seat I could see spurts of gray-white water jetting above the level of the opening. I stood up. "Sarelli—"

I thought he was coming to me—his eyes were on me all the way—but he walked past me and out his front door, closing it behind him.

With the bad arm and the bad leg, everything I did was awkward—getting into the suit, climbing over the sill. Somewhere in the process of pulling on sleeves, I got over one of those internal humps Sarelli had mentioned. Pain is a barrier when you draw back from it; not when you plunge in and breathe it deep. The next hump was supposed to be translating the pain, filing it under some other label in your brain, so that it didn't affect you the way pain does—but I didn't have leisure to work on that just now. Pumping up the bubble pressure helped; Sarelli was right again. It was like being wrapped in tight bandages, which for the moment felt good. I needed something to hold me together. The pain subsided to a burning ache, like a ragged red armband squeezing flesh and bone, and a tedious discomfort in my lower leg.

I limped to the open wall panel. The sill was almost at knee level. Spray freckled the suit skin just in front of my eyes. The River Bimran frothed and thrummed against the very wall of the building. Just alongside, water ran smooth in a trough of yellow stone that looked deep enough for comfort. This was what I'd wanted, wasn't it? Hadn't I shot the rapids of three separate mountain torrents on Kinsella, which is famous for its mountain torrents? And this was a better suit than I was used to, with skintight joint-cuffs dividing it into segments like an exoskeleton. I could bend and maneuver almost as easily as if I were naked, and the padding of dense air should cushion me against collisions. I raised my arms and dived in.

For the first moments the water took me, straight headlong down the slot. Then I was chuted up and over—fish leap, ski jump, carnival slide—up and down and into a booming capsule where I spun and battered against walls I couldn't see. *Don't flail,* I told myself. *Protect the head, never mind the arm, try to get the legs braced where they can exert a push.* I shoved off from the cupped rock wall, shoved against current and against buoyancy, shouldered, thumped, rounded a corner of some kind, and was poured suddenly down an underwater corridor striped with darker and lighter blindness. My lungs tugged gratefully at the pressing air. Noise roared around me, split by an occasional silken shriek. I slithered over sills and hurdles, under beams and jutting overhangs. I remembered the pain in my arm, and at the same instant my fingers slid into a dead-end groove, and the whole arm jammed against stone with a searing jolt. My ears rang, whether with my scream or with my silence. I dragged the arm out like a dead thing, and at once was tumbling out of control, back foremost, in the dark. I went through a long moment of insanity, knowing nothing except that I didn't want this. Sparks of light flared in my brain. There was nothing to hold on to. The blows that hammered me seemed to come from all directions. The air I tried to breathe was crushing me, flattening my lungs.

I could hold on to myself. I curled, fighting the dark and the pounding, retrieving my scattered arms and legs, forcing myself into a conscious ball. Pressure was my friend. I could breathe. I concentrated on the pain in my arm, sinking into it, making it another layer of pressure between me and the battering river. *Thank you, Sarelli,* I thought.

I noticed that my eyes were squeezed shut, and opened them. Pulses of light washed over me. The river was singing in deep-toned chords. Light meant up. Had I already passed the Center? Was I still in the midst of the city? Observational data, that was what I needed—something beyond the cries of the river and the tumult of light and dark melting and flowing around me and the insistent thumps that shook my pressurized person like importunate strangers in a crowd. *Rainbow Man,* they would be saying, if they spoke Galactic Standard; *Rainbow Rainbow Man Man.* I brought my knees to my chest and rolled, finding a passing wall to push against; failed the first time, tried again, and wasn't sure for a moment that I had succeeded. I uncoiled, righted myself, and part swam, part slithered through a lightening labyrinth. Knobs and patches of dark stone foam clung to sleek yellow columns—mementos of two different geological excitements. Some of that might have been happening here when I was a baby on the Trojan. An elbow of rock nudged along me, shoulder to ankle. I broke into air, looped my good arm through an arch of golden stone, and hung on.

Rainbows hovered like insects of light. *Well done, Sarelli,* I thought. Every good teacher should have demonstrations of basic principles handy. Everything changes—this nanosecond's stone is a different conformation of energy from last nanosecond's stone—but there are significant thresholds. Liquids flow. Solids just sit there. I hung on hard to my piece of solidity.

Straight in front of me, a plume of spray bobbed and wavered, carrying one of the rainbows in its crest. To the left, a smooth, transparent bulge, its surface glinting with

Bimran sunlight, hooded a knob of rock. But only its shape was motionless, and only the shape of the spray plume bobbed and wavered. Their bodies were moving water, flowing at so many meters per second, leaping, dodging, falling, reversing.

Through the spray I could see the bank, and nothing beyond it but the cloud-streaked sky. Wherever I was, I was past Northtown. I hoisted myself a little higher, scanning anxiously, and saw it with a thump of relief and hurt: the yellow walls of the Selection Center, still a hundred meters downstream, foreshortened from this perspective but unmistakable. I scanned the river and began to pick my way.

≈ 20 ≈

Unless proved otherwise, an individual is considered virtuous. The Selection system cannot function without hope.
                                        —*From* Revised Manual for Selectors,
                                                Working Draft, Chapter 2.

I was glad I'd climbed the bank—lower here and not so steep—before I peeled off the bubblesuit. Once released from the extra pressure, I felt limp and disjointed, like a broken toy. I stowed the bubblesuit in the empty footboard sling and picked my way across a stretch of rocky ground to the road. Floatcars passed me, turning into the entrance of the Selection Center—Bimranites coming to contemplate their future.

Nobody had told me which of the yellow cubicles was Doron's, but I walked straight to it. Its little garden was full of tall, frozen sprays, arching at the top. Even when the flowers are gone, the shape is beautiful. There was no entrance mat at the door. I hit it with my knuckles. Almost instantly it opened.

I stood face to face with Doron. "Redbeard tried to bring me in," I said. "We shot each other."

The look that washed across his face melted a fear inside me. No, I wouldn't have to argue with him. "Are you hurt, Liss?"

"Not too much to walk. The *Pilgrim* is leaving. Its lander lifts in half an hour. I came to get you."

He hesitated a moment, taking it in. "Where is—Redbeard?"

"Him and two others. I lost them somewhere near the Park."

His face was Doron-calm again. "I was just going out." He slid the door shut behind him and led me briskly down the walk and out the entrance. The nose of a footboard peeped out of his shoulder carry. He really had been about to leave his box. Starting a new case, maybe. One he'd never finish now.

But instead of taking the road, he touched my arm and steered me around the corner of the Center's exterior wall. Here on the river side, the wall stood head-high, closing us off from the buildings in the compound. "We can talk here," he said. "Don't worry, you have time to get to the spaceport."

"We," I said. "We have time. But we've got to hurry."

"I can't go with you, Liss. You must know that."

Something in me froze again. "Why not?"

"I'm a Selector. I can't run away from Selection." A statement of fact.

We stood face to face, the blank yellow wall of the Center on my right, the tumultuous river on my left. Everything sparkled; the river tossed freezing spray and flashes of reflected light indiscriminately on wall and pavement, on Doron's hair and beard, and the dull brown sleeves of my walkingsuit. Fragments of rainbow floated out of reach. *Words,* I thought. *Words are no good.* I took a step forward, leaning toward a kiss, and he blocked me with a lifted forearm. I stood still.

"I love you, Doron," I said. "But I hate what you do. I hate what you believe. I hate what you are."

My voice broke so badly on the last word, it was only a mangled lump of sound. He was watching me steadily, Doron's own open, level look, waiting to get it all straight. "What I—?"

"What you are." I shook, one momentary tremor, and it was over. Something was over. "I hate what you are," I said. After a moment I saw him take a breath—as if he would have said something if there were anything to say. "Don't *be* it," I said.

He looked away, turning his face toward the river. "I could say something like that to you," he said. He sounded far away already. But he turned back to me with a sort of smile. "You'd better go now."

"Come with me," I said. "We can work it out later."

A visible pulse of pain washed like a wave across his face. Children, they were all children. "Please," he said softly. "If you can help it. Please don't be angry at me."

I would have hit him if I'd thought it could do any good. "You're telling me to run away while you stand and face it," I said. "If I run, I'm leaving you to go to hell." He moved his head in that funny Bimran affirmation; he understood. "Is that the gift you want to give me? Remembering that I sent you to hell?"

"It's not certain," he said quickly.

"I left your copy of the *Manual* on board the *Pilgrim*'s lander. You've got to come with me, Doron. If they find out you gave away your *Manual*, it *will* be pretty certain, won't it?" So it was blackmail—it was blackmail in a good cause.

It did bring a flicker of new interest to his face. "I wish you hadn't done that, Liss. The *Manual* shouldn't leave Bimran.

But as far as my case is concerned, it doesn't matter. If there's an investigation, I can't hide what I've done."

A horrible chill went through me. *My case* didn't mean the case he was working on any longer; it meant himself as Redbeard's case, or somebody else's. "I don't like that, Doron," I said. "I love you. And I don't think I have the stupid courage—stupid courage is what it would be—to stay with you. You're asking me to choose between sending you to hell alone and going to hell with you. And you know what? I resent that."

He wouldn't have been Doron if he had been able to sidestep it. "In the worst possible case," he said levelly, "it's a choice between two being punished, or one. And it's more nearly purgatory than hell. It doesn't last forever, and we have reason to believe that in the end it does have a cleansing effect. After Punishment, death is always a blessing. Indeed, the Punished are the only humans who are guaranteed a happy death."

I hit him. I balled my left fist and cracked it against his mouth so hard that when I looked at my hand there was blood on it. "You shouldn't have said that," I said. My voice wasn't very steady.

It had snapped his head backward and knocked him off balance, so that he had to brace himself against the wall. Graceful even floundering. He wiped his mouth with one hand, but he didn't look at the blood. "And it's not as simple as you try to make it," he went on equably. "The danger to you is much greater than the danger to me. Punishment—" He hesitated. "I think Punishment would be harder for you to bear. You don't believe in it."

My hand hurt, throbs of pain like a heart beating. My ankle hurt, my bad arm hurt. Very minor pain, all of it, compared to what they were doing to people on the other side of that yellow wall. "There's a lot of uninhabited land on Bimran," I said. "We could make our own place."

"I could go with you," Doron said evenly. "Another planet, or a starship, or an island—it wouldn't matter which. Or I could kill myself. I've thought about those things. But I won't be guilty of that, Liss. I'll take the consequences of what I know."

"What you believe," I said. "I think your belief is a pile of shit, Doron. And if I thought there was a God like that, you can bet I wouldn't worship it."

His eyes looked wet-bright. *He's taken something*, I thought, with irrational hope. But he blinked, and I saw it was tears. "In a short time," he said, "a very short time from your viewpoint, you can be sure I'm dead. So it won't be long, you see."

"Just the rest of your life," I said. "And the rest of mine. The rest of my life I'll be thinking about the years of agony you died through while I was sleeking my hair one morning. Do you want to condemn me to that?"

I saw him swallow. His lips pressed together, and opened slowly. "You deserve it," he said.

I felt myself coming apart, my arm and my ankle giving up all pretense of solidity. I took one step forward and threw my arms around him. It hurt, both the step and the embrace, but nothing like what was hurting inside me. I pressed against him hard, trying to squeeze all pains to annihilation.

"Liss—" It was a groan of protest, or of something else. But I felt his arms around me, one quick hug before he broke away. "Liss," he said, the beginning of some unspoken sentence. Something had changed in his eyes. I had gotten to him. I had finally gotten to him.

"Will you come back with me to the spaceport?" I said.

"Yes," he said. "I'll take you there." He put his right hand into a pocket as if he didn't know what to do with it, and took it out again. He touched my cheek.

When I came back to consciousness—a sort of consciousness—I remembered the sick feeling of knowing that I was going under. "Where is he?" I kept asking Leona. And days later I was still going around the decks and corridors, trying to find by sheer persistence that there had been some mistake, that Doron was really on board somewhere.

By that time, of course, he was long dead.

"He brought you in just in time," Leona told me. "Draped over his back in a hoist-and-carry. They trained Selectors to do that, you know." Her old eyes looked bruised. Sarelli was dead, too; I couldn't check with him on self-rejuvenation techniques. "He lugged you in just before liftoff, so there wasn't much time for conversation. I only saw him coming because I was watching for you, hoping you'd turn up at the last second. Talking a lot to Rab and Hermes about it."

I touched my cheek. I thought I could still feel a little numbness. "How did he get me there? They were looking for me in the city."

"Who's going to stop a Selector? I suppose he may have had to flash his credentials once or twice." She scratched the side of her head. "One thing I have to tell you, Liss, and I hope it's all right with you. He asked very politely if he could look in your shoulder carry for something you had for him. Said you told him you'd brought it. Under the circumstances I didn't think I could say no. He found it first thing, right on top. Looked like a book, though he pocketed it so fast I couldn't swear to that. Said he'd loaned it to you."

"Yes," I said. "It belonged to him."

"Are you all right, girl?"

"What kind of a question is that?"

"Stupid. Stupid but friendly." She patted my arm. "I didn't smash you up like that on the riverbank, did I?"

I had forgotten my arm and my ankle. Somebody had fixed me up while I was out, but the patches still showed. "I'll tell you all about it sometime," I said. "There's plenty of time." I rubbed my cheek. "He wouldn't let me choose, Leona."

She snorted. "I thought Doron was always keen on people making their own choices."

"He was," I said. *You deserve it,* Doron had told me. But that was before he had put his arms around me.

"Live and learn," Leona said. "Which means you have to eat, Liss. You're lean as an Ishian condor. Come on and get a bite with me."

It wasn't revenge—not letting me choose, never letting me know how I would have chosen. Doron didn't approve of revenge. I fingered my cheek once more. "There's plenty of time," I said again, as if that answered something.